Tracks into Terror

Luke Hastings' life will never be the same again. One morning, just an hour after he leaves his Nevada farm on a simple errand, he finds himself involved in a complex plot to defraud the local silver mine.

Co-opted to act as deputy to an undercover investigator, Hastings scarcely has time to draw breath as a string of incredible and terrifying events unfolds before his eyes. Lead flies, trains are robbed in bizarre circumstances and people are destined to die. Before the culprits are finally brought to justice on a day of high drama a boy will become a man.

Tracks into Terror

MIKE REDMOND

Devon Libraries

A Black Horse Western

ROBERT HALE · LONDON

© Mike Redmond 2001
First published in Great Britain 2001

ISBN 0 7090 6941 3

Robert Hale Limited
Clerkenwell House
Clerkenwell Green
London EC1R 0HT

Typeset by
Derek Doyle & Associates, Liverpool.
Printed and bound in Great Britain by
Antony Rowe Limited, Wiltshire

Chapter One

The eastern foothills of the Sierra Nevada where the land folds gently down towards the arid wastes of the Sonora and Mojave deserts make passable farming country. Well below the winter snowline but sufficiently high above the desert floor to escape the relentless heat of summer, the pine-covered slopes of higher altitudes yield imperceptibly to pastureland criss-crossed with watercourses that originate up among the peaks and canyons to lose themselves, eventually, in the sinks and marshes that lie scattered along the western edge of the great desert.

Drummond's Crossing was one of a number of little communities to be found in the lee of the towering ranges that marked the final barrier to the westbound pioneers who had sought the fabled riches and benign climate of California during and after the rush of '49. It liked to call itself a township but a passing stranger with a more objective eye might simply have thought it little more than a cluster of ramshackle buildings along a dusty main street, servicing the sprinkling of farms and homesteads lying on the slopes to north and south. Some of the larger spreads sported fancy names such as *Ponderosa* or *Sierra Heights*, but most were more modest establishments, known simply by the name of the family who owned them and returning a steady, if unspectacular, living for their hard-working proprietors.

Early on a fine June morning Luke Hastings stood on the porch of one of these homesteads, hands in pockets, frowning across at the corral and the modest assortment of barns and sheds that represented the family premises – and wishing that it were ten times bigger. He had always fancied himself riding in through the gates of a ranch with the sign BIG H swinging impressively overhead, but a few hundred acres didn't entitle you to that sort of pretension – certainly not in these parts where everybody knew pretty well down to the last nickel what each of their neighbours was worth. A voice calling from inside the farmhouse snapped him out of his reverie. Hastings sighed, took his hands from his pockets and turned towards the door. Inside the main room which served as living-quarters and kitchen a tall middle-aged woman in a red gingham frock was standing behind a sturdy deal table wiping flour from her hands.

'You about ready, boy? Sure don't want to be tardy.'

Hastings grinned as he lifted his hat from a peg by the side of the door.

'Take it easy, Ma. I'll make it. Even if I don't, it ain't going to run away.'

Mrs Hastings grunted, gave her hands a final wipe and walked round the table towards her son.

'Maybe not – *of its own accord.* But folks is folks and they've been known to give things a helping hand.'

'I'm going to Drummond's, Ma. Not Chicago. Nothing ever happens there – not even a bit of horse-thieving, worse luck. There isn't even a lawman in town, it's so goddam peaceful.'

Mrs Hastings pursed her lips as she reached up to adjust the neckerchief neatly tied inside her son's shirt collar and button his leather vest properly.

'That's exactly what I mean – ain't nobody there to help you if you gets into trouble. So you look out for yourself and come straight back. Remember – you're carrying valuable cargo. My valuable cargo. And watch your language. Your pa wouldn't have taken kindly to his son using profanities.'

'Leave it off, Ma,' Hastings protested, shrugging off his mother's ministering fingers and taking a pace back towards the door. 'I only said *goddam*. And anyway, I'm eighteen now. I figure I don't need to talk like a kid all the time.'

'Only just eighteen. And you ain't a man till you acts like a man.'

Mrs Hastings' tone was sharp but her eyes were approving as she gave her son a final appraising stare. The loss of her husband last year following a kick in the head from a mustang he was trying to break had been a sore blow – both to her personally and to the fragile economy of the farm. But Luke, her only son, had stepped into the breach with an efficiency and willingness that did credit to his years and had already proved that as far as farm management went he had been his father's diligent pupil. He had inherited his father's looks, too. Tall, hazel-eyed, straight-nosed under a thatch of well-brushed dark-brown hair and already well-muscled from the exertions of farm work he could give a good account of himself in any situation, despite his youth. Still, there was no point in letting self-esteem become vanity. She reached forward and gave his hat a final admonitory tweak.

'You be off now and get it back here in one piece. It isn't much to ask.'

Hastings muttered 'Oh, shucks' under his breath and turned away before his mother could think of completing his humiliation by planting a farewell kiss on his cheek.

'And mind you stay out of that saloon, you hear?'

Hastings affected not to hear the final admonition addressed to his retreating back. He strode off the porch and walked across the yard to where the buggy stood waiting, with Streak, the farm's all-purpose beast of burden, already harnessed up. Hastings climbed aboard, flicked off the brake with the pointed toe of his boot, rattled the reins and said: 'Town, Streak.'

The horse pricked his ears and set off at a steady pace on to the track that led to Drummond's Crossing. No further command, or action, would be necessary on Hastings' part for the three-mile journey. Streak only had one pace – a leisurely walk – but in all other respects he was an ideal all-purpose farm horse, willing, reliable and perfectly capable of finding his own way into town and back without any guidance from his driver. That suited Hastings fine as it left him free to daydream a bit. He settled back and permitted himself another sigh.

In some respects today's errand was a nuisance in so far as it interrupted the routine of farm work. As his mother had quickly discovered, Hastings was a born farmer who never allowed himself to waste a day and had the seasonal, monthly, weekly and even daily routines of the farm ingrained in his working habits. A year ago he had assumed his father's responsibilities automatically – unthinkingly almost – because there had been no alternative. The farm had to be run, a living for himself and his mother had to be made, and he was trained for nothing else. And with no hired help the demands on his time were total – except perhaps at night in bed, when if he didn't fall asleep immediately, he sometimes allowed his mind to explore other paths and reflect on the opportunities that might lie out there somewhere in the wider world across the desert or the mountains. Which was why today's errand – although an interruption to his work – was not wholly unwelcome, even though he had made a display of reluctance when the envelope had arrived. A trip to town was a diversion, offering the possibility of conversation, news and – despite his mother's strictures – a visit to the one and only saloon where he intended to treat himself to at least one cold beer as a reward for his services. It was also a chance to have some time to himself and let his thoughts wander – leaving Streak to take care of the steering.

The arrival of the envelope had been an event in itself, for there were no mail deliveries to the farm. Correspondence was rare for farming folk anyway, and if they were expecting anything they collected it from the post-office in town. But the owners of the spreads neighbouring the Hastings also took it upon themselves to collect their neighbours' mail, if they were in town, and hand it on. Besides being an act of courtesy, it provided another much needed opportunity for people who otherwise saw little enough of each other to drop by and chew the fat.

So it was Walt Tanner who had stopped off last week and passed the envelope over to Hastings as he was wiring up fence posts in one of the outer pastures. Hastings took the envelope, saw that it was addressed to his mother, and pocketed it without comment – to Walt's evident disappointment, since there was an unspoken convention hereabouts that the delivery of a letter more or less gave you the right to know something about its contents – or at least who it was from. Hastings knew the answer to all that without even opening the envelope, but he didn't enlighten Walt – not because of any desire for privacy, but simply because he didn't want to spoil his mother's pleasure in letting the secret out herself when she was good and ready.

As Streak obediently headed the buggy in the direction of town Hastings patted the breast pocket of his shirt, reached inside his vest and pulled out the envelope. There was no letter inside. Instead he extracted a yellow printed form, now much creased from constant folding and refolding as a result of his mother's minute inspections, and checked its contents one final time – even though, like Mrs Hastings, he knew what it said off by heart. It was simply a copy of a consignment note from the Sears company in Chicago notifying that her order had been dispatched and giving details of its itinerary.

Since the completion of the transcontinental railroad and the improvements in communication it had brought, Mrs Hastings, like many farmer's wives out West, had become a devotee of mail-order catalogues. When her husband and son used to make sceptical comments about the time she spent of an evening sitting at the scrubbed kitchen table flicking through the pages of the latest catalogue under the glare of their best oil-lamp she would always reply tartly that it was better than reading a book – more like reading the Bible, really – because you could dip into it and leave it at any point and always find something interesting. There wasn't any plot to follow, and it didn't matter if you read the same thing over and over.

But up to the moment when her husband died Mrs Hastings had never actually ventured as far as ordering anything. Nobody of their acquaintance had – although rumour had it that after a series of lucky sessions at cards old Jake Hardiman, far out on the other side of Drummond's Crossing, had boldly ordered a new-fangled seed-drill and had been mighty pleased with it when it eventually arrived several weeks later.

Despite all the tempting goods on offer there was one particular page of her catalogue to which Mrs Hastings' fingers kept surreptitiously returning. It featured fully illustrated details and specifications of the latest Singer sewing machine. If she hadn't already heard through the grapevine about the marvels of these machines she would never have believed that they could actually do what the catalogue asserted they could. But even in the isolated communities around Drummond's Crossing there were people who had been as far afield as places like Sacramento or Salt Lake City and had seen the machines demonstrated. The only unwelcome piece of information in the relevant page of the catalogue had been the price that was being asked for the standard table model which she coveted, so Mrs Hastings had never confided her ambition either to her husband or her son.

When Joe Hastings had died, however, Mrs Hastings found herself in a position to indulge herself. Being a prudent man, Joe, knowing that he would have little cash to leave his dependants if the worst came to the worst, had insured his own life for the handsome sum of $100. This had provided his widow with the means to send Joe off with the best funeral the local carpenter/mortician could arrange and the means to turn to the end pages of her catalogue and at last fill in her order for the Singer machine.

Hastings leant back against the bench at the front of the buggy and smiled as he recollected the care with which his mother had placed her order. It was the first time he could ever recall her showing unrestrained enthusiasm for anything – possibly because it was the first time since her wedding that she had ever been able to have something that would be entirely her own. Hastings had offered no resistance to the expenditure even though the money might have been better spent on farm stock or equipment. Not only had the anticipation softened his mother's genuine grief and shortened her mourning, but he had to concede that there was a practical purpose to her purchase: she was already an accomplished seamstress whose occasional work was in demand locally. A sewing machine – if the catalogue's sales pitch was to be believed – would considerably improve her productivity. Maybe in time the investment could be recouped, but for now the important thing was to get the investment home. Neither he nor his mother had anticipated the unconscionable time that would elapse before they would receive news of delivery, but now the mail order company had made good and had even told them exactly when the consignment could be expected – hence today's excursion.

Drummond's Crossing owed its name to the fact that it was situated on a natural fording point where one of the old stage trails could cross Drummond's River and head further up into the Sierras. Stage traffic over the mountains had declined with the arrival of the railroad, and Drummond's Crossing might have become another ghost town had it not been saved by the railroad itself. Not the Central Pacific, whose main line was far away to the north, but the ambitiously named Truckee & Golden State Railroad whose proprietors had promoted it as a link along the eastern foothills of the Sierra Nevada all the way south into California. In practice money had run out after only thirty miles of track had been completed, but the railroad had survived as a sort of withered arm on the basis of the business produced by the silver-mines which had been developed some ten miles to the south of Drummond's Crossing and which relied on it as a link to the Central Pacific system further north.

Streak had completed about half the distance to town when Hastings heard, in the far distance, the prolonged whistle of a train engine. He glanced up towards the sun and nodded with satisfaction. Although he carried no watch he could see that the time must be approaching eight o'clock. The T&GS had no great reputation for punctuality but it looked as though the southbound train, which was scheduled through Drummond's Crossing on Thursdays and Fridays, was going to be on time. In an absent-minded moment of optimism Hastings flicked the reins over Streak's back but the horse made no variation in his pace. No matter, with over half the distance covered they would make it before the train anyway. Hastings resumed his day-dreaming. It occurred to him that he had never been further than about five miles in any direction from the farm in his entire life. One day when he had enough money in his pocket he would take a ticket on the northbound train, hitch on to the Pacific railroad and take it all the way to Sacramento. It would be nice to travel. . . .

As Hastings had anticipated, he and Streak made it to Drummond's Crossing before the train. There was no depot. The track ran parallel with what the commercial interests of the township liked to call Main Street until it reached a patch of wasteland conveniently adjacent to Calhoun's Livery Stables. There the trains stopped. Passengers were few and far between and freight business was equally slack, but the trains would have stopped anyway. By the side of the track there was a wooden water-tower where the boiler had to be refilled before the south-bound train could complete the journey to the end of the line at Virginia Springs. Hastings reined Streak in by the side of the stables. A whistle reverberated from further down the track telling him that the train was only minutes away. Such life as there was on Drummond's Crossing's Main Street continued without any obvious attention to the train's impending arrival. As far as Hastings could see, there were no passengers headed for Virginia Springs.

He was not surprised. The T&GS attached a passenger car to its trains purely as a formality and a matter of prestige – any profit was in the boxcars behind. As Hastings stepped down from the buggy, Hal Cummings, the rail-road's local agent who also deputized as telegraph operator, mail-office supervisor and general store proprietor appeared round the corner. Cummings paused, cocked his ear towards the direction from which the whistle had come, and consulted a large turnip-watch he had drawn from his vest pocket. Recognizing Hastings he inclined his head with a smile.

'On time today.'

'Glad to hear it.' Hastings returned his grin. 'You waiting for someone, Luke?'

'No. Some*thing*.'

He fished out the consignment note and handed it to Cummings, who read it carefully, lifted his hat, and scratched his head.

'Don't say nothing about it being on this particular train.'

'No, but we figure it ought to be. If it ain't, I'll come back tomorrow.'

'Sure.'

Before the conversation could continue a wagon driven by one of the local farm hands drew up nearby with some boxes headed for the end of the line. Cummings walked across to check over the paperwork, leaving Hastings by himself. Streak pricked his ears as another whistle sounded close at hand. Hastings craned his neck to the north as the train appeared from a bend in the track belching smoke. It approached slowly and drew to a halt with the engine directly under the water-tower. The crew jumped down, greeted Cummings and busied themselves with refilling the boiler. This and other formalities would keep the train here for at least half an hour.

As usual there was a passenger saloon immediately behind the tender followed by two boxcars. Hastings walked towards the rear of the train. As far as he could make out there no passengers in the saloon. He continued to the first boxcar and glanced around. Cummings was busy arranging for the farm wagon to back up to the rear car. To save time, and as the sliding door to the first boxcar was half open, Hastings decided to see for himself if his mother's expected crate was inside. He pushed open the door a little wider, gripped the edge of the car and swung himself up.

For a moment the contrast between the bright glare of the sunshine outside and the gloom of the interior left him sightless. He stood still for a moment until his eyes had adjusted and then looked around at the collection of cartons and packing cases of all sizes littering the floor. Trying to guess what size a crated sewing-machine might be, he approached a likely looking box and examined its label. No luck. An adjacent box proved equally unrewarding. Perhaps he would have to enlist Cumming's help to sort things out.

As he straightened up he caught sight of another crate about the right size perched behind a much larger wooden box whose lid had apparently come slightly adrift in transit. Hastings squeezed across and managed to make out his mother's name on the smaller box. With a grunt of satisfaction he grasped the corners of the crate to test whether it would be easy to manhandle across to the door. It proved heavier than he had anticipated. He took off his hat, laid it on the floor, wiped his forehead with a kerchief and took a step back so as to gain a better purchase on the crate. In so doing he knocked against the adjacent box, completely dislodging its lid which now slid to the floor.

With a muffled curse Hastings reached over to replace the lid. As he stared down into the contents of the box he froze momentarily and blinked as if confused by a trick of the uncertain light in the boxcar. He was about to open his mouth to yell for Cummings when something heavy struck him on the back of his unprotected head, sending him senseless to the floor.

Chapter Two

Mornings were generally quiet in Virginia Springs. The commerce that justified its existence was largely focused on the handful of mining companies scattered in the hills to the west of the railhead, and the ramshackle array of enterprises that lined both sides of its main street were largely devoted to serving the needs of the companies and their employees – especially on Friday and Saturday nights. Although the resident community of Virginia Springs was less than three hundred souls the town boasted three well appointed saloons. Here, right through the weekend, miners would drop in to blow their pay on liquor, women and gambling – regularly generating enough business to justify the premises standing almost empty for the rest of the week.

So Nick Travis was surprised when he arrived at the sheriff's office shortly after eight o'clock on a Thursday morning to find that his boss had had an overnight customer. The office was strategically well positioned within earshot of all three saloons so that of a weekend if you sat there with the door opened you could be pretty sure that you would hear trouble starting before anyone even needed to send for you.

It was the saloons that provided most of the business – drunks, fist-fights, card-table disputes. Nothing very serious, and nothing that couldn't be settled by throwing any offenders against the peace into one of the two cells that were attached to the rear of the office and letting them cool off till daybreak. Sheriff Turner maintained a policy of no sidearms in town so it was rare for the courthouse in remote Carson City to be troubled with any homicidal business from Virginia Springs. Whatever had to be settled was settled locally, and that was how the Sheriff and the companies liked it – it made for a quiet life and the minimum of paperwork.

Indeed, routine business was so easily dispatched that there would have been no justification for Nick's employment had it not been for the special nature of the shipments that were regularly being made in and out of town via the railroad. Bullion out and cash in to meet the companies' payrolls created a need for additional official protection beyond what could be provided by the companies' own security men, so they were content to subsidise the employment of an extra man in the sheriffs office. Turner himself was already a bit long in the tooth for any job that required the application of brain power or the expenditure of real energy so it suited everyone to have a younger troubleshooter on hand.

Travis had been in the job for nearly two years, having originally drifted into town to find employment as a security guard by one of the mining companies. Still in his early twenties, he took pride in his proven ability, his appearance and now his status as the number two law-enforcement officer in town. He never fastened his solid silver deputy's badge to his leather jerkin in the mornings without a smile of satisfaction, although of late his thoughts had begun to stray beyond the predictable routines of Virginia Springs to the opportunities that must surely lie open to someone of his experience in the wider world. In fact he was reflecting on this when he pushed

the office door open to find Turner standing facing the
bars of one of the cells, his arms folded, apparently deep
in thought.

'Morning, Jed.'

Turner took a second or two to snap out of his reverie
before replying.

'Customer.'

He jerked his head towards the cell, where Travis could
make out the figure of a man stretched asleep on the
wooden bench which constituted the cell's only furniture.
The recumbent figure had his face turned towards the
wall, so Travis was unable to make out his identity. Turner
glanced at the clock on the wall.

'Past eight. Best wake him up. Usual way.'

Travis nodded, grinned, and made his way out back.
For, a moment there was no sound other than that of a
pump being vigorously worked, and then he reappeared
with a wooden bucket in his hand. Turner produced a
bunch of keys and unlocked the cell, but the noise failed
to disturb the sleeping occupant. Travis entered the cell
and pitched the contents of the bucket directly at the
sleeper's head. He stood back with satisfaction as the
freshly pumped water produced its intended effect. The
sleeper snorted, gasped, came rapidly to consciousness
and sat up choking.

'What the . . .'

The rest of the sentence was cut off by a burst of coughing as he tried to rally his thoughts. After a few seconds he
pulled himself together and swung his feet on to the floor.

'Travis, you lousy sonofabitch. Whaddya do that for?'

Travis, who had now recognized the overnight guest as
an old-timer who ran (not very successfully) a small farm
some four or five miles to the north, dropped the bucket
on the floor and stood back slightly, his slim figure carefully blocking the cell door as usual in case the occupant

should contemplate a sudden unauthorized exit.

'Just givin' you a wake-up call and an early morning wash all in one go, Jim. Saves time for all of us.'

'The hell it does, you skunk.'

The dripping figure stood up unsteadily, tried without success to brush some of the surplus water off his shirt and pants, and squinted at his jailer.

'You lettin' me outta here? I got a day's work to do even if you ain't.'

Travis shrugged but maintained his position in the doorway with one arm braced against the cell bars.

'Depends on the sheriff. I don't know what you're in here for.'

'Drunk and disorderly,' said Turner. 'Very drunk and very disorderly. You ought to know better, Jim Purvis. Specially on a Wednesday night.'

Purvis stared at him for a moment.

'Yeah? What's Wednesday night gotta do with it? I'll have a few drinks any night if I feel like it.'

'Fine by me. Just as long as you don't go shooting your mouth off disturbing the peace. Man in your position ought to know how to handle his liquor.'

Purvis rubbed his head in bewilderment. 'Shootin' my mouth off? I can't remember . . .'

'Exactly,' said Turner. 'You was babbling half the night. Thought you'd never shut up. Amazing what liquor does to a fellow's tongue.'

Purvis grunted but made no reply. Then he jutted his jaw aggressively towards Travis. 'So what you staring at, dude? You gonna stand there all day?'

Travis glanced around at Turner who nodded almost imperceptibly. Then he stepped to one side to allow Purvis out of the cell.

'Your hat's behind the door, Jim,' said Turner. 'No charge this time.'

'Thanks for nothing.'

Purvis retrieved his hat, clamped it firmly down on his sodden head and put one foot on the wooden sidewalk outside. Then he turned with a frown as though he had only just absorbed what the sheriff had said.

'What did you mean about babbling? I don't remember nothing except complaining about the way they short-measure your whiskey in the Silver Slipper.'

'Yeah,' said Turner. 'That as well. Now git.'

Motioning to Travis to see Purvis off the premises he sat down at his desk with his feet propped on a spittoon that always sat at a convenient and well-measured distance nearby. Travis closed the door behind Purvis, crossed the room, perched himself on a corner of the table which served him as his own desk and studied Turner's face for a few seconds. The early morning sunlight was streaming in through the window behind the sheriff's head, leaving the profile nearest Travis well lit, while the other was curiously shadowed. Turner, momentarily unaware of Travis's inspection, toyed ruminatively with a silver paper-knife. The sunlight reflected off the streaks of grey which ran through the sheritff's hair and glinted on the heavy gold signet ring which adorned the little finger of his left hand.

Travis found himself speculating, not for the first time, on Turner's age. All he knew about him – since Turner himself never volunteered any information – was that he had been around as town lawman for the last ten years or so, having originally come to the area in the rush that had followed the opening of the Comstock Lode in the late '50s. The sudden finding of gold on the eastern side of the sierra had sparked off the same sort of speculative fever that had followed the great discovery of gold at Sacramento in '49, but despite frantic efforts the Nevada side of the mountains had never yielded the steady stream of gold of which so many dreams were composed. Instead, it was silver that kept the miners busy. Nobody made fortunes, but the profits were regular enough to keep the paycheques coming. How, or when, Turner had made the transition from pioneering to law enforcement nobody exactly knew, but as Virginia Springs had grown his office had grown with it so that now he and the town were almost synonymous. Nothing happened there that he didn't know about – and if the citizens of Virginia Springs had ever bothered with the niceties of mayoral elections Turner would have been a tough candidate to beat.

At least, mused Travis, he would have been in the old days when Turner's energy had matched that of a growing community. Now, as he studied the sheriff's pursed lips and the lines on the side of his face nearest to him, etched more precisely by the glare of the sunlight, he had the impression that the sheriff had aged almost overnight and that instead of the vigorous administrator of law and order with whom he had worked amicably for the last two years he was suddenly looking at nothing more than a tired old man. He waited for a moment to give Turner the opportunity to comment on their recent guest, but as the sheriff seemed disinclined to open the conversation Travis took the initiative.

'Kind of strange to find Jim Purvis here as a cell guest.'

Turner did not reply immediately. Instead he reached across his desk, selected one of the special half-corona Cuban cigars which he obtained through an importer in San Francisco, lighted it and inhaled with an almost sacramental reverence. Travis, who smoked nothing more ambitious than cheroots, found this early-morning habit tiresome, but had long ago accepted that the sheriff would have to be indulged in this minor folly – despite the inevitable fogging of the atmosphere in the tiny office. Having removed the distinctive foil band from the base of the cigar, Turner finally got round to answering Travis's question.

'Found him measuring his length on the floor of the Silver Slipper just before midnight. Seemed kinder to haul him in here for the night rather than stick him back on his horse. He'd never have made it back home in that state.'

The shadow of a frown passed rapidly over Travis's face. Turner had explained what Purvis had been doing in the cell, but it still wasn't clear why he had been drinking in the first place.

'Seems kind of strange he should act like that,' Travis persisted. 'He's not what you'd call a regular as far as the saloons are concerned. And I've always thought he could hold his liquor.'

'Well, it takes all sorts,' said Turner. As if to discourage any further idle speculation he stood up and reached for his hat.

'Guess it's time for my breakfast. Mind the shop for a bit, Nick. Come and find me at the Parlour when you've finished.'

'Sure.'

As Turner walked out Travis stretched, opened the window to dispel some of the tobacco haze, walked over to the desk and idly leafed through the few papers that required attention. Nothing to engage his interest. He sighed and turned towards the window, thrusting his hands deep inside his pockets. Contemplating the prospect of another well-ordered day doing nothing in particular in Virginia Springs he watched Turner's retreating back as he made his way across the street towards the only eating place in town. For some reason everyone called it the Parlour, although the fascia board clearly proclaimed it to be the VIRGINIA SPRINGS DINING ROOMS.

Travis continued staring for a moment or two, and then recalled himself to duty. One of the less agreeable aspects of his job was to see to the general tidiness and cleanliness of the office and the cells. He turned reluctantly away from the window and cast an appraising eye over the premises. Nothing much had happened over the last twenty-four hours to disturb the well-ordered appearance of the office, but one cell had been occupied and would need attention. He walked into Jim Purvis's recent accommodation, retrieved the wooden bucket, refilled it at the pump outside and returned with the bucket in one hand and a broom in the other. For reasons both of economy and hygiene the cell had been furnished with nothing more than the slatted wooden bench on which Purvis, along with so many others previously, had spent an extremely uncomfortable night. It was easy enough to sluice it out with a bucketful of water. Indeed, reflected Travis, as he flung the water against the rear wall of the cell, the job had been half done already when he woke Purvis with the traditional cold douche. He was just taking up the broom to sweep the water towards a small drainage hole in the side wall when he noticed a scrap of folded paper which had floated out from beneath the bench.

Thinking at first that it might be a greenback which had dropped out of Purvis's pocket during the night Travis bent down to pick it up. On seeing, however, that it was simply a small sheet of writing paper he was about to consign it to the broom when his curiosity got the better of him. Wiping the surplus water off the outside of the paper with the cuff of his shirt he unfolded it carefully. The ink-written sentences inside were untouched by the water, but the uncertain light in the cell which only possessed one small barred window at head height, made them difficult to read, forcing Travis to retreat to the office window. He studied the writing for a few moments, and then folded up the paper and placed it in the breast-pocket of his shirt.

Having returned to the cell to complete the cleaning out process, Travis clamped his hat to his head and stepped outside. Virginia Springs was slowly stirring into as much life as you could expect to see there on a Thursday morning, but some improvement might come with the arrival of the morning train which always created a bustle of activity. Travis stood for a moment savouring the fresh pine-scented early-morning air and then headed off towards the Parlour, his high-heeled boots clattering on the worn timbers of the boardwalk which stretched from either side of the office.

Travis glanced down at the Mexican leather of his toecaps and noted with displeasure that they were flecked with dirty water from the recent discharge of his duties. He took much pride in his appearance, and one of the small perks of his office was his ability to order one of the lads down at the livery stables to apply the necessary amount of polish and elbow-grease to restore a respectable shine. For the moment, however, appearances could wait.

Travis crossed the road and pushed opened the Parlour door. Only a couple of tables were occupied. Travis recognized the depot superintendent and a couple of his staff engaged in their breakfast. Madge Wilkins, the proprietress, cook, and waitress of the establishment finished refilling a coffee-tup and turned towards him. She nodded in the direction of an empty table.

'Take your pick, be with you in a minute.'

Travis shook his head. 'Ain't here to eat. Looking for the sheriff. He been in here this morning?'

'Ain't seen him.'

Madge paused with the coffee-pot in one hand and glanced at the longcase clock which stood against the rear wall of the room.

'Kind of unusual. Sheriff likes to keep regular hours.'

'Yeah,' Travis agreed. 'Well, no matter. If he shows up tell him I was looking for him.'

'Sure.'

Outside. Travis paused to look up and down the street but could see no sign of Turner. A block or so beyond the dining-rooms the street began to break up into a random collection of stables, sheds and warehouses clustered around the railhead. Travis put his head into the general store and one or two other places where the sheriff might have called, but nobody recollected seeing him. Figuring that he might as well be thorough, but with no great expectation of success he decided to complete his reconnaissance by checking out the railhead. 'Railhead' was the preferred T&GS description of the end of the line, but it tended to overexaggerate the reality. Virginia Springs happened to be the point where the company had run out of the money to construct further – so there the line just ran into the sand. A couple of short sidings had been built alongside and were usually occupied by the one or two dilapidated boxcars occasionally brought into use for exceptional shipments of freight or mining equipment. The end of the line itself was marked by a wooden turntable alongside a water-tower and timber-shed. Apart from that the only appurtenance of a railroad station was a small lineside clapboard office which served as ticket-window, dispatch-point and telegraph terminal.

Hands thrust deep in his pockets Travis picked his way carefully through the dust, horse-manure and general detritus which littered the end of the street. Joel Bentham, the resident representative of the T&GS would likely be around, even if the sheriff wasn't, and was always good for five minutes of inconsequential gossip – sometimes even real news if he had picked anything up from the wire. Travis entered the railhead yard and made his way round to the office door. To his satisfaction, through the glass panes he could see Jed Turner's bulky figure standing by the desk. He pushed open the door and walked in.

'Came lookin' for you at the Parlour, but as you weren't there I thought I'd try the railyard.'

Turner wheeled round abruptly as Travis spoke, almost as though taken by surprise, his right hand poised over his pistol holster.

'Oh, it's you.'

Travis smiled as he observed Turner's right arm tense and then relax. 'Sorry if I scared you.'

The sheriff s reply was gruff.

'Kind of reason to be jumpy, I guess. Called in to talk to Joel, but I didn't expect to find this.'

Turner stood to one side, giving Travis a clear view of the desk. Joel Bentham was sitting in his shirtsleeves at his accustomed place, his right hand stretched out towards the telegraph apparatus. All appeared normal except for the red stain on the satin lining of his vest where a knife had been thrust deep between his shoulder blades. As Travis stared at the unexpected tableau Turner summarized the situation in one laconic sentence.

'Looks as though Joel's transmitted his last message.'

Chapter Three

Luke Hastings opened his eyes and tried to establish some control over his senses. At first his only perceptions were those of alternating flashes of light and dark and an all-pervasive rumbling noise. Then tactile sensations began to take over. He was lying face down on a dusty wooden floor which obstinately refused to stay still. Every few seconds it jolted violently, sending spasms of pain through his head. Hastings groaned and felt cautiously up to the focus of the pain on the back of his scalp. As his fingers located it he yelped aloud with the sudden sharp discomfort of the contact and let his hand fall back to the floor. Now he knew where he was, but for a few moments he made no further attempt to move as he allowed himself time to marshal his thoughts coherently. He was flat out on the floor of the boxcar where he had been examining the packing-cases. But now the train was moving and the flashes of light were coming from the open doorway as the train passed through patches of sunshine and shade. The boxcar had not been designed for human comfort and his ears were filled with the sound of rattling, grinding bogies and axles as the train made its ponderous way along the poorly graded track. He groaned again and, fearing that he might not have enough strength to stand up, contented himself with rolling over on one side to give his eyes a chance to focus better.

He had fallen with one of the wooden walls of the boxcar at his back. The rapid alternation of light and shade was confusing his vision so he blinked several times in an effort to clear it. After a few moments he became aware of the figure of a man, silhouetted by the light from the open doorway, sitting close by on one of the cases. Hastings raised himself painfully on one elbow so as to get a better perspective, but the man's face was in shadow and all but invisible to him. He grunted as Hastings shifted his position.

'Took you long enough to come round. You must have a skull like paper. I only tapped you.'

The combination of the laconic tone of the voice with the continuing pain in the back of his head had the instant effect of rousing Hastings from a state of total passivity to one of righteous indignation.

'Why, you son of a . . .' he gasped, scrabbling with his hands to obtain the necessary purchase on the floor to lever himself upright. But before he could improve his position his assailant had leant forward and grasped hold of his boots, forcing him to remain in a sprawled position with his back against the side of the car.

'Try moving again, mister, and I'll slug you hard enough to put you out for the rest of the ride.' He sat back and tapped the Colt nestling in his belt. The gesture was unmistakable: obviously it had been the pistol which had inflicted the damage on Hastings's scalp. The boy's rage at the injustice of his treatment, however, momentarily rendered him impervious both to the threat of further attention from the Colt and to the blinding pain in his head. With an oath he kicked out with accuracy at the man's groin, dislodging him sideways from the packing case. Before he could recover his balance Hastings had stumbled to his feet and launched himself, fists flailing, at his persecutor. With the temporary advantage of surprise he succeeded in landing a few good punches in the man's ribs, but in his weakened condition it was scarcely a fairly matched contest. His adversary rolled adroitly to his feet and exploited a momentary lurch of the boxcar as the train rounded a bend to launch his fist into Hastings's solar plexus. As Hastings gasped desperately for breath he found himself being hauled upright by the collar and thrust painfully backwards against the side of the car. His vision disintegrated into myriad flashing stars and the ache in his head splintered into a thousand shards of agonizing pain as a gloved hand swiped left and right across his face until he slumped once again, semi-conscious, to the floor.

When he came to again, he became aware that the other man was kneeling beside him unknotting the kerchief that Hastings kept tied around his throat. As the man eased his head forward to examine the wound in his scalp Hastings recoiled instinctively as though anticipating another series of blows, but found himself restrained by a strong pair of hands on his shoulders.

'Easy, mister. I was just trying to assess the damage. Ain't no call to pull away from me.'

This time the voice was gentler, with no hint of implied violence.

'Ain't no call to go on knocking me around,' protested Hastings. 'I haven't done anything wrong.'

'That so? Matter of opinion, maybe.'

Reassured by the conversational tone of the man's voice that there was no immediate physical threat Hastings sat forward and tried to rally his thoughts as he surrendered to the careful application of the kerchief against his bleeding scalp.

'Look, mister, who are you? If you're a company man I

swear I wasn't trying to steal anything. I was just collecting something, Here, I can prove it . . .'

Hastings fumbled in his pocket for the consignment note, but found his hand abruptly knocked back to his side.

'I'll ask the questions, youngster. And we'll take them nice and easy. You make any move without my say-so and you know what you'll get. First off – what's your name?'

'Luke. Luke Hastings.'

'All right. Where you from?'

'Drummond's Crossing.'

'What do you do there?'

'I'm a rancher.'

This reply provoked a snort of derisive laughter. 'That so? And you no bigger than an overgrown schoolkid. What's your pa do, then?'

'I ain't got a pa. He died last year.' Hastings's voice had dropped perceptibly with this reply, but he continued with sullen obstinacy. 'And I *am* a rancher. Leastwise . . . I'm a farmer, at any rate.'

'All right. Now what do you want to show me? And move your hand real careful.'

This time Hastings was allowed to produce the consignment note. The man took it and edged closer to the door in order to get enough light to read it. As he stood framed against the doorway Hastings at last had an opportunity to study him properly. He was hatless, aged somewhere in his mid-twenties, Hastings guessed, with a firm decent-looking expression under thick curly black hair. He was dressed in conventional Western style with checked shirt, denim pants supported by a thick leather belt, and a pair of well-made boots – but there was something in his voice and complexion that belied the superficialities of his appearance. Life out West always made its own special imprint on people – if only because of the extremes of climate and the hardships of earning a living – and it was immediately clear to Hastings that his interrogator had his roots elsewhere. From the paleness of his complexion and the evenness of his accent he was probably from somewhere out East. More than that Hastings couldn't speculate, but it made the circumstances of their encounter that much more intriguing.

'Looks like your story checks out,' said the stranger, handing back the paper. Hastings took it and then paused in mid-fold, staring at him wide-eyed with consternation. For now he had remembered exactly what he had been doing at the moment when he had been struck on the head. Unwilling to risk another confrontation by attempting to stand up he drew himself back against the wall, one knee raised and both hands flat on the boards. The expression on his face must have been transparent, however.

'Something worrying you?'

Hastings remained dumb for a moment and then pointed shakily over to the large packing case from which he had dislodged the lid.

'The case . . . I was looking in the case . . . when . . .'

'Sure you were. Care to verify what you saw?'

The stranger held out his hand to help him up.

'Come on . . . no need to be shy.'

Hastings stood up reluctantly. The other man allowed him a moment to find his balance and then led him over to the case. The lid had been replaced.

'This the one?'

Hastings gulped and nodded.

'What did you reckon you saw?'

Hastings hesitated before forcing out a reply, uneasily aware of the rough justice that the railroads were reputed to hand out to trespassers on their property.

'Mister, I reckon I saw a . . . body.'

'That so?'

The stranger placed a hand on the lid and shoved it sufficiently to one side to reveal the contents of the case. Hardly daring to breath Hastings leaned forward. There, just as he remembered, lay the crumpled and blood-stained figure of a man. He glanced up uneasily.

'Is he dead?'

'He was when I heaved him in there about an hour ago.'

Hastings felt the events of the last few minutes threatening to overwhelm him. The blow on the head, the abortive fist-fight, a dead body in a packing case, the relentless motion and noise of the train, the total confusion of his senses all combined to produce a feeling of nausea. He wiped his forehead with his shirt-sleeve and shot a longing look at the open door.

'I feel kinda sick, mister,' he mumbled.

'Be my guest.'

Hastings stumbled, gagging, towards fresh air, but as he reached the door the train hit a sharp curve and the sudden lurch of the boxcar caused him to miss his footing. In a moment he had measured his length on the boards, head towards the door – and now the cant of the train as it continued round the curve impelled his body across the dusty floor so that before he had even had time to yell he found himself almost half out of the doorframe, scrabbling frantically for any sort of handhold to prevent himself from being ejected on to the track. With all thoughts of vomiting abruptly removed from the immediate agenda, Hastings actually allowed himself a split second to wonder whether he might just as well roll out and take his chance on a soft landing – the train, despite all the noise, was scarcely making fifteen miles an hour. But now the curve straightened out and the trackbed all but disappeared as the train rumbled on to a timber trestle-bridge over a ravine – leaving Hastings staring down into a hundred-foot abyss. Opening his mouth to yell, he felt a sudden hefty tug at his waist as the stranger, bracing himself with one hand against the doorframe, grasped his belt and exerted enough strength to prevent him from sliding any further. For a moment or two, as Hastings stared helplessly down through the timbers of the bridge at a raging torrent far below, the contest between gravity and brute force seemed evenly matched and ready for decision either way. But as the train reached the other side of the bridge the cant of the track reversed, the floor of the boxcar pitched slightly upwards, and Hastings slowly slid back to safety.

With Hastings thrust securely back against a packing-case, and the other man reclining opposite him, both took a few minutes to recover their breath. The stranger spoke first.

'You sure like excitement, by the looks of it.'

'Depends.'

Hastings permitted himself a slight grin. All traces of nausea had miraculously vanished, and – with the unanticipated forced intake of fresh air – so had most of the ache in his head.

'Guess I owe you a thank you, mister.'

'Wouldn't come amiss.'

There was a further silence and then Hastings said, 'Yeah, but look, I can't thank you if I don't know your name. I already told you mine.'

'All right. You can call me Scott.'

'That a first name or a surname?'

'Whatever. Just call me Scott.'

Hastings considered this, opened his mouth to protest at the incomplete information, thought better of it, and, instead, held his hand out to be shaken. The man called Scott accepted it with gravity and gave it a firm shake. Chewing his lip, he stared at Hastings as though trying to come to a decision. Then he spoke again.

'I'm kind of impressed, kid. I crack you on the head, smack you around a bit, tell you I just stuffed a man in a crate and you sit there wanting to shake hands. You been in this sort of situation before?'

'No. And don't go calling me no kid. I'm eighteen.' Scott inclined his head in mock obeisance.

'I apologize . . . Luke. But like I say, I'm impressed. You reckon you can handle yourself?'

Hastings shrugged.

'I can make out.' He grinned again. 'In fact I like a good scrap. Don't get the opportunity for much practice around where I live, though. I landed a few good ones on you, didn't I?'

'Right. Pity you're not armed, though. Fists don't count for much.'

'Mister . . . I mean, Scott . . . none of us carry guns around Drummond's Crossing except shotguns, maybe. Ain't no call.'

'Ever handled a Colt? asked Scott, extracting the pistol from his belt and tucking it out of sight inside his shirt.

'No sir,' Hastings grinned again as he put his hand to his scalp, 'but I sure know what they can do at short range.'

Scott chuckled. 'You'll do.'

He reached into his vest pocket, extracted a gold half-hunter, flipped it open and checked the time.

'Listen, we've got about half an hour before this old rattletrap reaches Virginia Springs. There's a few things I want to tell you,'

'But I . . .'

Scott cut Hastings' protest off with a wave of his hand.

'Just shut up and hear me out. When I've said my piece you can make your own mind up about what to do next. Just because I'm up against it, there's no need for you to be. Or of course you can jump off. We ain't going that fast.'

Hastings affected to give this option serious consideration before shaking his head.

'Kind of a long walk back – or forwards, come to think of it. Guess it makes sense to stay put for the time being.'

'You aren't afraid I'm going to send you home in a packing-case?'

'You could have booted me out of the door just now when we were going over that bridge. I'm willing to take a chance. Anyway, I'm kinda curious. I want to know why you stuffed a dead man in a crate.'

'Then settle back and listen. His name's McCabe. I'll even tell you why I stabbed him.'

Chapter Four

Nick Travis shouldered his way through the batwing doors of the Silver Slipper saloon and paused to survey the scene. The deputy sheriff's mood was sombre and slightly tetchy. Joel Bentham had been something of a fixture in Virginia Springs for as long as anyone could remember. He had been an affable old-timer with a fund of stories and anecdotes which he was ready trot out at a moment's notice – a characteristic which Nick had appreciated on days when he himself had nothing in particular to do and other entertainment was in short supply. Bentham was the last man in the world to make enemies, so if Travis hadn't seen the situation with his own eyes he would have been hard pressed to believe that Joel would end his days with a knife thrust in his back.

That accounted for Travis's sombre mood. He had counted Joel as a friend. But the murder meant work for the sheriff's office – and tedious work at that. Even a cursory inspection of the body had revealed that the death had occurred within the hour – a fact confirmed by Doc Maguire when summoned post-haste from his breakfast. As there was no evidence of a dispute or violent scuffle in the office and as, inevitably, no one had seen or heard anything suspicious, there were no obvious leads. Which meant that there was going to be a lot of routine investigation to do. Some of it had fallen immediately to Travis.

Since Bentham had no known enemies amongst the townsfolk there was an immediate presumption – at least in the sheriff's stated view – that his death must be down to outsiders, for reasons as yet unexplained. So Travis had got the job of scouring the town for unfamiliar faces. Hence his tetchiness. As the town boasted no hotel as such, the obvious places to start were the three saloons: any stranger almost inevitably fetched up at one or the other of them. His enquiries at the Silver Horseshoe and the Silver Garter had yielded little of interest. One or two cattlemen passing through, a couple of drummers doing the rounds with their samples and order-books, none of them with guilty demeanours or blood on their hands. This was going to be an unrewarding assignment.

The Silver Slipper was as lifeless as the other saloons at mid-morning. Rusty, the barman, was standing at one end of the counter polishing glasses, while at the other stood the proprietress, Ruby Jessop, sorting her way through a pile of cash, presumably last night's takings. She looked up from her counting as Travis's high-heeled boots sounded on the rough wooden floorboards.

'Get you something?'

Travis shook his head. Another of the perks of his job, besides having the local stable urchins at his command, was the willingness of the town saloon-keepers to supply him with beer on a slate that was never called in – the unspoken agreement being that the sheriff's office was always on hand to sort out any trouble on demand, without making difficulty for the saloons themselves or interfering with their business.

'Not now. I'm here on business.' Ruby nodded her head. 'Yeah, I was kind of expecting you.'

Travis permitted himself a wry grin as he leant with one

arm on the counter surveying the rest of the room.

'News travels fast around here.'

'You should know,' said Ruby. 'There ain't much of it most of the time. Makes anything unusual something to talk about.'

She pursed her lips, and closed the cash drawer.

'Sorry to hear about old Joel, though. Don't make sense for something like that to happen to him. Seems kind of difficult to imagine anyone having a grudge against that old fellow.'

'That's what I reckon. But someone thought it worth-while to stick six inches of silver paper-knife in his back.'

Ruby's eyebrows arched slightly. 'That how it was done? We got a real skunk around here.'

'His own paper-knife, too. Makes it seem kind of worse, somehow.'

'Sure.'

Travis exchanged gossip with Ruby for a minute or two, taking the opportunity whilst doing so of inconspicuously casting a professional eye over the Slipper's mid-morning clientele. There was no one else standing at the bar, and only a few tables were occupied. Most of the customers were regulars with familiar faces – old-timers who had nothing better to do than sit around making one beer last all morning. Only at one table were there a couple of figures whom Travis did not recognize as locals, although somewhere at the back of his mind lurked the feeling that he ought to be able to identify them. Carefully avoiding eye-contact he turned back to the bar and addressed Ruby quietly from the corner of his mouth.

'Two fellows at the rear table. They been here long?'

As she replied, Ruby, imitating the professional disin-terestedness of Travis's demeanour, affected to arrange some bottles against the mirrored display-stand behind the bar.

'Came in yesterday. Ain't seen them before. Paid for their room up front – no trouble.'

'They been here all morning?'

'I reckon. Ordered a real ranch-hand's breakfast up in their room earlier and they've been down here ever since.'

'What number?'

'Four, next floor up.'

Their eyes met conspiratorially in the pier-glass mirror. Without turning round Ruby added, 'Best use the back stairs. House key's in the usual place.'

With a final unobtrusive glance to ensure that the two men were not about to move, Travis straightened up, made his way round the side of the bar, collected the master key from its usual hook beside the kitchen door and made his way up the back stairs to Room 4. Nothing unusual met his eyes when he opened the door. The uncleared remains of a breakfast were visible on a table by the window, there was a spittoon on the hearth containing an empty whiskey-bottle and a couple of cigar stubs, and the men's few belongings were draped on the various items of furniture. They were obviously travelling light, with little more than could be stored in a saddle roll. Having satisfied himself that there was nothing in the room that need engage his professional attention Travis closed and locked the door, and then made his way downstairs.

'You sure they ain't been out of here this morning?' he asked as Ruby gazed at him with an expression that mixed curiosity with irony.

'Sure as I can be. I took their breakfast up myself well before eight, and they can't go out of here without anyone seeing them. That right, Rusty?'

She turned for confirmation to the barman.

'Right.'

Travis sighed. He knew he could rely on them to tell the

truth. They would be as anxious as anyone in town to nail Bentham's killer. He was about to leave it at that and start a trawl of the town's other commercial enterprises when he recollected himself to his duty. Sheriff Turner was a stickler for detail – even the most trivial detail – and if it turned out that two strangers were in town he would at least expect Travis to be able to report who they were and where they were headed. He pulled himself up to his full height and walked over to where the two men were sitting engrossed in conversation over their drinks.

'Howdy.'

The men broke off their conversation and looked up as Travis loomed over them. Neither spoke. Travis thrust his left thumb into his vest pocket below where the silver deputy's badge was pinned as if to make sure that the men had noticed his official status. Their demeanour remained unchanged, however, with no particular additional indication of respect.

'You guys just got in?'

The silence that followed this question gave Travis a moment to study their faces. Both were young – probably in their early twenties – clean shaven and dressed in the usual trail gear. There were no distinguishing characteristics about either of them as far as he could see. Both had their hands on the table with no visible bloodstains on their fingers or anywhere else. In any case, as he had protested to Turner when assigned to this particular duty, was it likely that a stranger would commit a murder and then sit around town waiting to be picked up? Logic dictated otherwise, but Turner had insisted on the procedure being carried out, arguing that at least it might turn up some useable information. At last one of the men spoke in a tone which made it clear that the question was resented.

'Last night.'

'Staying long?'

This time the second of the two answered.

'Any particular reason for asking, mister?'

Travis shrugged. 'My business to know who's coming and who's going. Now, would you care to answer the question?'

'We ain't staying. Fixing to be riding out late this afternoon.'

'OK. The lady behind the bar says you've been here all morning. That right?'

'Sure it is. Look, what is this, mister? Kind of unfriendly around here, isn't it?' Travis returned the young man's aggressive stare with a jut of his chin.

'Not particularly. It's just that we had a spot of trouble in town this morning and me and the sheriff kind of like to know who we're entertaining as guests – especially when it concerns the death of one of the townsfolk. . . .'

There was a moment's silence as Travis allowed the two men to digest this information. They frowned at each other and at him, but there was no indication of guilt or complicity in their expressions.

'So perhaps you'd give me your names. Just for the record, that is.' One of the men half rose from his chair, muttering an oath.

'Goddamit, why in heck should we . . .'

But the other laid a restraining hand on his arm.

'Easy, Jeff. Deputy's only doing his job. Ain't no call to take it personal.'

'The heck there is,' mumbled the other, subsiding into his chair again. When he spoke again his voice was sullen, but he complied with Travis's request.

'Jeff Booker. And my pardner's name's Pete Brodie. Anything else you need to know?'

'Guess not. Thank you gentlemen, Enjoy your drinks.'

He tipped his hat ironically in their direction and then

turned back to the bar. Suddenly he felt tired and confused. Ruby's offer of a drink was mighty tempting, as was the chance to do a bit of thinking in the cool of the saloon. But that particular pleasure would have to be postponed for an hour or so while he continued his enquiries along main street. With a nod to Ruby and the barman he made his way out into the brilliant sunshine. . . .

Brodie and Booker stared in silence at Travis's retreating back but made no comment until his steps had receded into the distance on the boardwalk outside the saloon. Then Brodie tipped his glass unobtrusively towards that of his companion with a tight smile.

'If that's the measure of the law in this here town I don't reckon we got much to worry about. Did you see the dude's boots?'

Booker swallowed his whiskey in one relieved gulp.

'Yeah. Wonder if he ever gets them real dirty.'

They sniggered companionably for a moment.

'Figure he suspected anything?'

Brodie shook his head. 'I reckon we sounded straight enough. Why, I didn't bat an eyelid when you said we was riding out this afternoon.'

'No reason to,' said his companion, shortly. 'It was truthful enough, in its way. Weren't no business of his how exactly we're riding out.'

'Yeah.' Brodie grinned into his empty glass. 'Care for another?'

Booker considered this suggestion, but shook his head.

'Ain't no time for serious drinking. Cormack's expecting us to get this right. In any case if everything pans out it'll be champagne in Sacramento tomorrow night – worth waiting for.'

The shadow of a frown passed fleetingly across Brodie's forehead.

'Jeff, you reckon Cormack's read this one right? I mean, it all seems a bit weird to me – rummest job I was ever asked to do.'

Booker stared at him across the table. When he spoke his voice was subdued but full of menace.

'Why, Pete, you wouldn't be having second thoughts would you? Cormack's usually well enough informed. Of course, if it's all too big for you, you should have . . .'

'Shut up will you? It isn't too big for me. It's just that it all seems too . . . well . . . too simple.'

Booker chuckled.

'All the best jobs are simple. That's the secret. Keep it simple and there's less to go wrong. . . .'

Nick Travis's morning had been as unproductive as he had feared. News of the murder down at the railyard had spread through the town like wildfire, and there was no shortage of speculation about possible motives and suspects. None of it was of the slightest interest to him. What was in short supply was hard facts. Nobody had noticed anything unusual or seen anybody acting suspiciously. Tired and hot, with the day well advanced, Travis found himself at Wilkins's Livery Stables which was the last set of commercial premises on his list of visits. There was no sign of activity in the yard. Travis walked across to the main stable building where the door stood half open.

'Matt around?'

Travis addressed a young boy who had shouldered a load of hay prior to distributing it to one of the stalls.

'No sir.' The boy dropped the hay in a feed-basket, brushed his hands on his dungarees and turned to face Travis. 'Mr Wilkins got a call to go up to the Dryden spread. They got a mare having trouble foaling.'

The deputy sheriff recognized him as one of Wilkins's regular unpaid juvenile assistants who hung around in the

hope of picking up tips from satisfied customers. The boy
cast a hopeful glance down at Travis's boots, on which a
fine layer of town dust had now overlaid the original stray
splashes of dirty water from the cell floor.

'Give you a shine?'

'Yeah. And put some beef into it.'

As the boy bustled off in search of polish and cloths,
Travis made himself comfortable on some bales of hay
with his back propped against the wall. Half-way along the
row of stalls there was a familiar nicker as his own horse, a
chestnut gelding with an irregular splash of white down
his muzzle, recognized the sound of his voice. Travis whistled softly in reply.

The boy returned, settled himself at Travis's feet and
applied himself to the boots. Travis eased his hat off his
brow and let his thoughts wander over the morning's
events – glad of an opportunity to do some quiet thinking.
The boy had other ideas, though.

'You gonna need Blade, Mr Travis?'

'What?'

Travis frowned momentarily as he jerked his thoughts
back to the boy's question. 'Your horse – you want me to
saddle him up for ya?'

'Oh.' Travis stared at the boy's upturned face. 'Yeah,
guess you can at that. Reckon I've done enough walking
for one day. But you finish these boots real good first.'

'Yes, sir.' The boy applied himself with renewed vigour
as Travis absent-mindedly jingled a few coins in the pocket
of his pants. A double tip could be anticipated.

A few minutes later, with his boots restored and Blade
saddled, Travis settled his hat on his forehead, mounted
and dropped a few coins into the boy's outstretched hand.

'Thanks, Mr Travis.'

'Nothing to it. Must be your lucky day – two jobs in a
morning.'

'Sure thing. But better than that. . .' The boy reached in his vest pocket and produced a quarter. 'I made that just before you turned up. Two guys ready to ride out wanted their horses.'

Travis stared down at him. 'What two guys?'

The boy shrugged. 'Don't rightly know. I ain't seen them before. Must have ridden in last night.'

'You hear any names?'

The boy scratched his head. 'I think one of them was called Pete,' He returned Travis's stare. 'Anything wrong, Mr Travis? They sure acted normal enough.'

'Mind your own business, youngster.' Travis turned Blade's head, ready to ride out of the yard, 'I suppose you didn't see which way they headed.'

'Yep, took the trail towards Drummond's.' He laid his hand on Blade's bridle. 'That information worth anything extra, mister?'

'Riding your luck, huh?' Travis reached down and flicked the boy's ear. 'Tell you later maybe. . . .'

'Yessir.' The boy grinned and massaged his ear as Travis set Blade into a trot. He stared after the retreating figure of the deputy sheriff with an expression of resignation on his face. Some people enjoyed all the action. . . .

Travis was puzzled and suspicious. If the two men who had ridden out were the same as the two he had spoken to in the Silver Slipper – and they almost certainly were – they had been less than honest about their intentions. There was nothing to connect them with the killing at the telegraph office, of course, but it would be useful to shadow them for a while – if only to make sure that they were quitting his territory. Trailing them would be no problem if they were only ten minutes or so ahead. Blade was the sort of horse that always liked to be somewhere else, so once his head was set in the right direction you could rely on him to cover the ground smartly.

Following the same general direction northwards to Drummond's Crossing, the trail wound through sandy ground shaded on both sides by the thick pine-woods that covered the lower slopes of the foothills. Travis was no expert tracker, but traffic was light on this particular trail, and he had no difficulty in picking out the recent tracks of two horses in the sandy shale. Evidently the riders were in no particular hurry, as the evenness of the hoofprints indicated nothing more than the pace of a leisurely jogtrot.

After a mile or so the track ran level with the railroad and then separated at the head of a shallow ravine where the railtrack continued level on a trestle bridge while the trail ran below, forded a shallow river and then climbed through the woods on the far side. As the trees closed in again, providing some welcome shade from the mid-morning sun, Travis sat back in his saddle, allowing Blade to set his own pace. He was just reflecting that although he might be engaged on a wild-goose chase it was at least preferable to an afternoon spent asking vain questions in the heat of town, when he suddenly became aware that the hoofprints he had been following had petered out.

With a muffled curse he pulled Blade up and dismounted to examine the ground. It took only a few seconds to confirm that his inattentiveness had lost him the trail. Nothing, either hoofed or wheeled, had passed through here in either direction recently. To punish himself for his nonchalance Travis declined to remount, but simply took Blade by the bridle and began to retrace his steps, searching for the point where his quarry had left the trail. Now, of course, the task was rendered less easy by the fact that the track had been further disturbed with Blade's spirited trot, so greater concentration was required.

It was a full half-mile before Travis discovered where he had gone wrong. At a curve in the trail both sets of prints diverged to the left and disappeared upwards into the thickly wooded slopes. Travis remounted. To the right he found himself looking down through the trees towards the trestle bridge and the trail descending under it from the other side of the ravine.

He was on the point of congratulating himself on picking up the tracks again with such little difficulty when it occurred to him with a sudden pang, that anybody who had been up here at the moment when he approached on the far side of the ravine would have had a clear view of his approach if they had happened to look back. He was just wondering whether he was suddenly in danger of becoming the hunted rather than the hunter when there was a flash of fire from somewhere in the trees above him and a bullet sliced through the crown of his hat, ripping it from his head and sending it spinning into the dust. . . .

Chapter Five

Luke Hastings rubbed the sore patch on his scalp and stared at Scott in bewilderment.

'You stabbed him?'

'That's what I said.'

'But . . . why?'

'Because if I hadn't, I'd be in that crate instead of him.'

Hastings took a moment to digest this information.

'I see, so . . .'

'No you don't.' Scott's reply was curt. He chewed his lip for a couple of seconds as if pondering where to start, and then continued. 'You know anything about silver mining?'

Hastings shook his head. 'I told you, I'm a rancher . . . er, farmer . . . not a prospector.'

'Right. But you know there's silver lodes all over Nevada territory?'

'Oh, sure. There's one where this train's headed right now.'

'Exactly. Owned by a company called Conglomerated Mining – otherwise known as CMC.'

Hastings nodded his head, 'Yeah, I heard of it. Keeps Virginia Springs pretty busy by all accounts. Must be real profitable.'

Scott chewed his lip again and paused before replying.

'Used to be, *Should* be. But that's the problem – it isn't.'

'Lode running out, eh? They say it happens all the time.'

'Nope. Plenty of silver. But . . . well, let's say it isn't as profitable as the management thinks it ought to be.'

'That so? So why don't they . . .'

Scott leant forward and rapped Hastings' thigh again.

'Hush up a bit, will you, Let me do the explaining. The mine's local, but Conglomerated Mining isn't. It's owned by a group of bankers in Chicago. Let's just say that it's come to their attention that they're not getting quite the same output that they were getting a year or so ago, even though they've got the same number of men on the payroll. Bankers don't necessarily know much about mining, but they sure know how to read a balance sheet. And what they're reading at the moment has turned them a tad suspicious.'

Hastings drew his knees up to his chin and leant forward with eyes now wide open with attention and interest.

'You mean, they figure someone's swindling them.'

'Something like that.'

'So that's . . .'

'So that's where I come in. I'm here, as you might say, on an exploratory mission to find out what's going on.'

'Gee. You one of those guys that work for that outfit . . . what's it called?' Hastings paused as he ransacked his memory for some casual information he recollected seeing in a copy of one of the rare newspapers that had penetrated to the Hastings spread. 'Punk . . . Picker . . .'

'Pinkertons, you mean.'

'Yeah, that's it.'

'No, but it's the same sort of thing. Investigating. In secret.'

Hastings sighed with satisfaction as a piece of the

mental jigsaw puzzle that had been troubling him fell into place.

'I guessed it might be something like that.'

Scott frowned. 'You're fresh up from a one-horse farm. You couldn't have guessed anything.'

'Well, I guessed you're no Westerner. I'm right about that, ain't I? I figured you was from out East.'

'Yeah? Well I guess I'll just have to keep working on my accent.'

'Weren't your accent that set me thinking – it's your clothes. You wear them like an Eastern dude even though they're all messed up.' Hastings chuckled. 'Why, you even got creases in your pants.'

Scott scowled down at his pants and then grinned.

'All right. You got me. Nice to know I'm not dealing with a complete hayseed.'

Hastings grinned in return.

'I ain't no hayseed, but I still don't . . .'

'You still don't know what you're doing in a boxcar with me and a dead man in a crate. Right. It's quite simple. I came out from Chicago a week ago and started my enquiries on the Pacific Railroad. The bullion – what there is of it – gets from there to Chicago all right. So the obvious point to pick up the trail was at the railroad junction. Didn't take me long to find out where the . . . ah . . . leakage was happening. Here, let me show you something.'

Scott stood up and beckoned Hastings over to a wooden crate bearing the stencilled initials CMC on all sides. He pulled back the lid.

'Take a look at this.'

Hastings peered cautiously inside, half expecting to be confronted with another folded corpse. Then he relaxed.

'So? It's empty.'

'Right. Because this is the return trip. On the way out

from Virginia Springs it's filled with silver bars.'

'OK, but then . . .'

'The problem is . . .' Scott continued, almost as if talking to himself, 'what you see isn't necessarily what you get. Here, take a closer look.'

He tipped the crate on to one side so that the base was visible. At the bottom all four sides were apparently reinforced with an additional slat about six inches in width to provide extra stability. Scott reached into his belt and extracted a short Bowie knife with an elaborately carved handle that Hastings took to be a turquoise inlay in the Indian style. He used the tip of the blade to prise away a small stud that appeared to be securing one end of the reinforcing slat on the uppermost side and then, to Hastings' astonishment, slid the piece of timber deftly backwards to reveal a cavity about three or four inches high extending through the base of the crate. He turned to Hastings with a wry smile.

'Impressive, huh? Like one of them Chinese puzzle boxes, but much bigger.'

'Jeez,' Hastings muttered. 'So that's . . .'

'So that's where the . . . shall we say . . . unofficial output of the mine is going. The rest gets to Chicago as usual – after our friend in the crate and his crony in the Central Pacific depot have removed their slice of the action.'

'Wow, you're real smart, mister.'

Hastings stared at Scott for a moment with unfeigned admiration, but then his brow furrowed again.

'But . . . so why didn't you arrest them, then?'

Scott shook his head. 'Son, I'm an investigator, not a lawman. I ain't got no rights to be arresting anyone. Besides, the job isn't complete. I was hired to track down a swindle, and it's clear enough that it starts up in Virginia Springs. Someone up there's organizing it – stands to reason. There's paperwork to be fixed and men to be bribed. Couldn't happen otherwise. That's what my employers want to know. Then the law can take over.'

Hastings nodded. 'Guess that makes sense. But wait a minute . . .' He stiffened suddenly and backed away. 'If you ain't got lawman's rights, how come you killed McCabe?'

Noting the tremor of anxiety in Hastings' voice Scott smiled in reassurance. 'It wasn't part of the plan. I was planning to ride up in the boxcar to give myself time to figure these crates out. Train's just about to get under way while I'm examining the crates when he jumps me. I thought he was safe away in the passenger car. Pulls this pretty little knife on me, I wrestle it off him and let him have it. Didn't have much choice really. Better for him to spill his guts than spill the beans. . . .'

Scott paused, scanning the mixture of emotions that were reflected in Hastings' guileless features.

'You finding all this a bit much to take in?'

Hastings made no immediate reply, but distanced himself from Scott by returning to his place near the open door and seating himself against the wall.

'Kind of.'

'Pity. Something tells me I may be in need of help when we get to Virginia Springs. But if you don't feel up to it you can always skedaddle out that door.'

'Ain't no call for me to skedaddle anywhere,' riposted Hastings sharply. 'I haven't done nothing wrong.'

'Sure thing. You can just sit it out here and ride all the way back again. After they've dealt with McCabe's body of course. You might be required to provide the local forces of law and order with a little background information.'

Hastings considered this jibe in silence. 'Looks like it isn't as straightforward as I figured.'

'Quite. But I do need your help. And remember, I took

a chance on you way back. I didn't have to tell you anything.'

Hastings considered this remark in silence as well – half wishing that Scott had never told him anything. As it was, he seemed to be involved whether he liked it or not. But wasn't it just this morning that he'd stood on the farm wishing for something to happen out of routine? And now it had – with a vengeance. He gathered himself and set his jaw.

'All right. You got me hooked, mister. But if you've been stringing me along I'll . . . I'll get real riled up. So what's next?'

Scott smiled. 'Easy. I was going to suggest tipping McCabe out of the car. He's kind of an encumbrance where he is.'

Hastings stumbled to his feet again.

'Hey, I can't tip him out on the track – even if he *is* dead. Don't seem kind of fitting, whatever he's done.'

Scott, who had risen with him, laid a hand on his arm.

'I said I was going to suggest tipping him out, but then I had second thoughts. Like you said, it don't seem kind of right. Still, we've got to keep him out of sight – we don't want to upset the welcoming committee.'

'Welcoming committee? What welcoming committee, for Pete's sake?'

'I wired the mine this morning to tell them not to make any more shipments until I arrived. Someone'll be expecting me.'

'With a six-shooter if they know what you're up to.'

'No. With a red carpet. As far as the big wide world is concerned I'm the company's agent. In a way, it's true. Now, let's deal with McCabe.'

'But how. . . ?'

'Kind of obvious isn't it? If it sticks in your craw to pitch him overboard, we'll have to nail him back in the crate.'

Hastings ran his hand through his hair, wincing as he inadvertently touched the wound on his scalp.

'Jeez, you're a cool son of a . . .'

'Have to be in my profession. Just find me the lid, will you?'

Hastings picked up the lid while Scott stuffed straw gathered from the boxcar floor round and over the folded corpse, effectively concealing it from first view if any one peered inside the crate. They replaced the lid and hammered back the nails with the heel of one of Hastings' boots.

'That's that,' said Scott, dusting off his hands. 'Now we've got to decide what to do with you.'

'Whaddya mean, *do with me*? I'm stepping off with you, aren't, I?'

Scott stroked his chin. 'I think not. I'm expected, you're not. So you'll be more use where nobody can see you. The swindle's being run either from the depot in Virginia Springs or from the mine – or possibly both. We'll start with the depot – which means getting you inside unseen. So how to do it. . . ?' He stared speculatively at the scattered crates lying around the car, Hastings, following the direction of his gaze, put out a hand in protest.

'Now wait a minute. I ain't no corpse and anyways I wouldn't fit no . . .'

'Of course you would – supple body like yours. Anyway, it wouldn't be for long – just till you was inside the depot.'

'Aren't you overlooking something? They'll be expecting to unload empty crates. Won't it be kind of obvious that there's something inside?'

'Sure. But a couple of these crates are packed with legitimate equipment and supplies sent from out East. We pitch out the contents and put you in instead.'

Ignoring any possible protest, Scott had already moved across the car examining labels to identify the loaded crates. Finding one, he turned with a yell of satisfaction to Hastings who was still skulking in the shadows.

'Well come on then. We've only got ten minutes.'

They manoeuvred the crate towards the open doors, prised off the lid and began to pitch the contents on to the track. When the crate was empty Scott peered into it with satisfaction.

'Plenty of room for you as long as you keep your knees bent.'

'Yeah?' Hastings' reply was less than enthusiastic.

'Sure. Now get in, will you. I've got to nail the lid back on.'

'Now wait a minute, wait a minute,' protested Hastings in rising tones of panic. 'I've gotta get out of that darned thing, How am I going to do it if you've nailed me in?'

Scott sighed. 'Jeez, you youngsters . . . here, take this.' He handed Hastings the Bowie knife that had belonged to the late McCabe. 'You can use it to lever the lid off. The nails should come out easy enough if I hammer them back in the original holes.'

Hastings took the knife as gingerly as if being offered a rattlesnake to stroke, and thrust it into his belt.

'Mind you don't cut yourself,' remarked Scott with a heavy trace of irony which Hastings, in his nervousness, completely failed to notice.

'I can handle a knife, mister. I was brought up on a farm, remember?'

He climbed into the crate and managed to fold himself around the perimeter without too much trouble. Scott beamed down at him.

'Great. See you later – wherever. . . .'

Before Hastings could change his mind he slammed on the lid and hammered the nails back into position. Hastings found himself in pitch darkness, with the rattling of the train reduced to an imperceptible rumble somewhere underneath his head. He shifted in momentary panic and banged his fist on the side of the crate.

'Hey, Scott. You keep an eye on this thing, ya hear?'

'Don't worry.' Scott's voice, given a slightly booming quality through the resonance of the hollow crate, seemed surprisingly distant already. 'I'll catch up with you in the depot.'

'Whaddya mean, in the depot? I thought you're supposed to stick with me all the way.'

'Wake up, Hastings. I already told you – someone'll be expecting me. *As a passenger.* Won't do my story much good if they see me climbing out of a boxcar when the train stops.'

'But . . .'

'But nothing. I'm heading forward.'

Hastings hammered on the crate with increasing emphasis. 'Scott, you sonofabitch. You better not leave me, you hear? We're partners, aren't we?'

'Sure thing, Luke,' said Scott reassuringly. Then he added in an undertone calculated not to penetrate the plywood walls of Hastings' temporary prison: '*But not necessarily equal ones. . . .*'

Disregarding the continuing sound of Hastings' fists on the sides of the crate Scott swung himself out of the open doorway and grabbed hold of the vertical iron stanchion that ran as a handhold parallel with the outer side of the doorframe. Leaning out to ensure that the train wasn't about to negotiate a sharp curve he braced one foot against the door-handle and used the stanchion to raise himself till his head was level with the cantrail that ran along the side of the roof. Grasping it with both hands and a silent prayer that the train would maintain its even course he laboriously hauled himself on to the roof.

A series of long hoots from the engine up front indicated that the train was approaching its destination. The speed had dropped to around ten miles an hour, but, even so, Scott had difficulty maintaining his footing as he manoeuvred his way along the roof-boards to the front end of the swaying car. Much to his relief his descent was made easier by a ladder of narrow iron staples hammered horizontally into the leading face of the car. Having negotiated these without difficulty he paused to catch his breath for a moment above the rattling couplings and then launched himself across to the shallow balcony edging the outer platform of the passenger-car. Climbing over he checked himself for damage, lifted his hat to smooth his hair, wiped his sweat-stained face with his neckerchief and was brushing the last of the boxcar dust off his shirt and pants as the train rounded a final curve and made its way into Virginia Springs.

Positioning himself calmly at the edge of the platform Scott surveyed his point of destination for all the world like a tourist embarking on a long awaited vacation. As the train ground to a halt, with clanking metal and hissing steam giving way to a sudden profound silence, Scott cocked an unobtrusive ear to satisfy himself that Hastings had stopped hammering. Then he stepped down into the yard and looked around expectantly for whoever was supposed to be meeting him.

Chapter Six

Instinct combined with experience came to Travis's rescue – otherwise he would never have survived the second shot. As his hat skittered into the dust he kicked free of his stirrups, siderolled out of his saddle, hit the ground and flattened himself in the shelter of a shallow outcrop of rock by the side of the trail. Simultaneously a spurt of fire and the whang of a bullet crumping into a tree behind him gave him notice that whoever was up there was shooting in deadly earnest. Suppressing a curse of self-reproach for his carelessness he remained flattened and motionless for a few moments while trying to take mental stock of his situation.

The debit side of the ledger was as uncomfortable as his physical position. For a start he was quite sure that the shots had come from a rifle – a Winchester, by the sound of it. Since Travis had nothing but his sidearms, that gave his ambushers an immediate long-range advantage if there was going to be a shoot-out. His thoughts turned agonizingly to the one and only carbine – a much cherished but little used Springfield – which he and Sheriff Turner kept locked up in their office back in town, but there was no point in wasting time regretting his failure to bring it along. The first priority was to test whether the rifleman up above could make out anything of his body.

Travis's head and torso were well under the lee of the rock, but his legs were sprawled out on to the track. However, there had been no third shot, so perhaps the shooter was unsighted by the steep angle from which he was firing. Travis eased his right hand down to his holster in an attempt to dislodge his Colt. It would be no match against a rifle, of course, but having it in his hand would make him feel a little less naked. His fingers made contact with the butt and he concentrated on easing it out of the holster without making any conspicuous arm movement. He was aware that the shooter would no doubt be shifting his position to get a better view of his quarry and loose off another shot, but all instincts to make a grab for the pistol had to be sternly suppressed.

After what seemed an eternity, during which he hadn't even dared to breathe, Travis felt the Colt loosen and come free of the holster. He was just permitting himself the cautious reflection that at least now he would be able to shoot back – even if not very effectively – when a third shot sliced through the heel of his outstretched boot. The force of the impact wrenched sharply at Travis's ankle but his yelp of pain was smothered by a snap and an explosion of dust as the shell lodged itself in a stone just beyond his foot, sending slivers of flint in all directions. Blade, who had remained standing nearby during the brief action, suddenly whinnied in pain and surprise as a shard of stone struck hard into his left fetlock. Then he reared and bolted for safety into the trees on the other side of the track.

There was no time to regret the temporary loss of his horse. The momentary distraction of Blade's abrupt departure gave Travis his one and only chance of extricating himself from an impossible position. As the horse wheeled away in a flurry of dust he launched himself to the side of the rock and rolled into the undergrowth. As a fourth shot slammed viciously into the spot he had just left, Travis picked himself up and flattened himself behind the trunk of the nearest spruce. He might be outgunned and unhorsed but at least he was upright, with a gun in his hand and some means of getting a sight of his attackers. It was the first entry on the credit side of the ledger. . . .

But only a nickel entry, he reflected after a minute or so in which he had waited in vain for some sound or movement from the trees above him. True, he wasn't pinned under a rock, but all the advantages seemed to lie firmly with the other side. He couldn't retreat backwards without exposing himself, he'd lost his horse, and there was little chance of any passing stranger appearing on the road to provide assistance. He was just wondering whether he might have to sweat it out like this until nightfall when a voice hailed him.

'Hey mister. You hear me? Come out with ya hands up. You know you're pinned.'

Travis stiffened. The voice, somewhere up ahead of him within the cover of the trees, seemed surprisingly close – maybe less than a hundred yards. If so, someone was getting over confident. Distance gave the rifle advantage over the pistol; but someone seemed intent on throwing that advantage away. If it came down to less than fifty yards Travis's Colt would be on combat terms with the Winchester. He waited a full minute to maintain the suspense before replying.

'That so? Then why don't you come and get me?'

Travis cautiously edged his face round the side of the tree in an attempt to get a sight of his assailant. Almost immediately there was a loud report as a rifle-shot sent slivers of bark from the tree-trunk just inches above his head showering into his face. Travis loosed off a blind shot just to make it clear that he had fire-power at his disposal – but with no hope of hitting a target. The only encouraging fact, he reflected as he withdrew fully behind the safety of the tree, was that the rifle-shot had clearly been delivered at fairly close range.

'Nice try, mister,' he jeered. 'Pity ya didn't have your spectacles on.'

There was no reply. And as the reverberations of the interchange of gunfire died away Travis, without daring to expose himself again, listened intently for the slightest sound of movement up ahead. After a minute or so the faintest trace of a dead twig being snapped underfoot gave Travis his chance. It was now or never. He stiffened momentarily, and then, crouching so as to put the level of his head below his opponent's probable line of fire, thrust himself from out behind the tree firing a covering shot as he did so.

For a second he got a brief glimpse of the other gunman in the shadow of a tree less than thirty yards distant. And as anticipated another rifle-shell whanged accurately past the spot where his head should have been. Travis had shot blindly again, but he had aimed at nothing specific. By drawing the other man's fire he had given himself a couple of precious seconds to extricate himself from another impossible position. As the shell cleaved the air over his head he launched himself away from the tree into the shelter of some friendly undergrowth and then scuttled, still semi-crouching, through ferns, shrubs and bushes until he had achieved higher ground somewhere behind where he calculated the last rifle, shot had come from.

Now, as he once again became the hunter, there was less need for caution. Peering through the greenery, Travis could see the gunman crouching in the shelter of a tall spruce clearly uncertain as to which direction he ought to be pointing his rifle. Travis wondered briefly how many more shots the guy had at his disposal. By Travis's reckoning he'd loosed off six already, and people didn't ordinarily go around with pockets filled with boxes of rifle-shells. Still, there was no point in speculating. In any case Travis's own ammunition situation was strictly limited. He'd set out with both of his six-shooters with full chambers, and just half a dozen rounds in his gunbelt. Eighteen shots in all and two gone.

Travis grimaced and concentrated on the job in hand. He actually had sight of his opponent, but with the uncertain light cast by the sun flickering through the canopy of the evergreens and the necessity of firing from a crouching position he couldn't be sure of achieving a lethal shot. And, of course, he would only have one chance, as by firing he would then have given his position away. Somehow he had to give himself an extra edge.

Sweating profusely Travis scrabbled about frantically in the soil around him until his free hand made contact with a medium-size stone. With infinite care, while still trying to keep his opponent in sight, he transferred his pistol to his left hand and used his right to prise the stone from the ground. As it came away, he hefted it securely in his fist and launched it in an accurate parabola to land with a flurry of dust on the ground just ahead of the tree where he had recently been pinned.

The rifleman spun round and levelled his weapon in the direction of the disturbance, giving Travis the chance he needed. Springing out of the bushes he sprinted as noiselessly as possible through the trees and was levelling his Colt at the man's back at less than ten yards before the fellow had had time to register his mistake. Travis was tense and angry, but as his finger tightened on the trigger, somewhere from beneath his bubbling emotions came the restraining impulse of the West's unwritten code of chivalry. Had the man been facing him Travis would have fired without compunction, but in the space of just one second he became aware that he couldn't shoot a man in the back at point blank range. Instead, almost as if in a dream, he heard himself saying:

'OK, you sonofabitch. Drop the rifle and stand up real slow with hands above your head.'

In case his opponent had any illusions about the reality of the turned tables Travis carefully clicked back the hammer on his Colt. The unmistakable sound, as deadly a threat as the rattle on the end of a rattlesnake's tail, produced its desired effect. Without turning to face him the man let the rifle drop to the ground.

'I'm doin' what you said, mister. Don't shoot, The rifle ain't loaded, anyway. I've run out of shells.'

Travis stepped smartly forward and slicked the gunman's sidearm out of its holster. 'OK. Now turn around.'

Face to face at last, Travis recognized Brodie from their brief encounter at the Silver Slipper.

'Guess you got some questions to answer, Brodie.'

'Yeah?'

'Yeah. Like why you think it's all right to take pot-shots at a lawman, not to mention tellin' lies about your intentions back there in Virginia Springs.'

'Maybe I don't like being trailed for no reason. And anyway, I couldn't see who you were.'

'That so? Well, that's something we need to talk over – but this ain't the place to do it. I'm taking you in.'

'Sure thing, Mr Deputy Sheriff. You gotta horse?'

Brodie's hands were still raised, but there was something in the tone of his voice which suggested that he was less than impressed with Travis's powers of authority. That and the sudden realization that Brodie was staring past him instead of looking him in the face caused Travis's heart to leap into his throat. He had been so busy dealing (successfully, he thought) with the intricacies of disarming a rifle-shooter that he had clean forgotten that he had been following two men, not one. As the sweat broke out anew on his forehead a voice spoke behind him with a sinister chuckle.

'Sure he's got a horse. He just doesn't happen to have it handy.'

Travis made to turn round but the muzzle of another rifle in the nape of his neck made him freeze.

'Drop the guns Mr Deputy Sheriff, and put your hands up.'

Travis recognized Booker's voice speaking a foot or so from his ear. He let the pistols fall to the ground and slowly raised his hands as Booker continued to speak.

'Pete, why don't you lighten his load a bit by relieving him of his other gun as well?'

'My pleasure.' Brodie grinned as he removed Travis's remaining Colt from its holster and collected the other firearms from where they had fallen. Travis felt the pressure of the rifle muzzle released from his neck as Booker walked around to face him, his lips opened in a sneer.

'Anythin' you'd like to say, Mr Deputy Sheriff, before I blow your head off?'

'Sure is,' said Travis, trying to keep his voice even. 'And – just for the formalities – my name's Travis. Or you can call me *sir* if you prefer.'

'Let the sassy lawman have it, Jeff. We ain't got no more time to waste.'

Affecting to ignore Brodie's intervention Travis stared coolly at Booker's face, contorted behind the sights of his rifle as he levelled it at Travis's head.

'You fellows make a habit of killing lawmen as well as telegraph operators?'

'Our habits ain't no concern of yours, Travis.' Booker's finger tightened perceptibly on the trigger. 'Let's just say we don't take kindly to being trailed when we're minding our own business. Pity you didn't mind yours.' Then he continued, mimicking Travis's precise way of speaking, '. . . *and just for the formalities* we ain't killed no telegraph man.'

'OK. But that's just the point, isn't it? As far as I was concerned you hadn't done anything wrong until you loosed off a shot at me. That's not a hanging offence, even if I was disposed to make something of it – which maybe I'm not. But killing a lawman's something else. You fancy having your faces splashed around on Wanted posters all over the territory? Sooner or later you'd be hunted down whichever way you went – east or west.'

Brodie stepped up level with his partner and thrust his hands in his belt. 'Smart talker, ain't he? But *sir*'s forgetting something.'

'That so?' said Travis cocking his head in Brodie's direction.

'Yeah. Like . . . there don't appear to be no witnesses around here. Ain't nothing to connect you with us.'

'Except the kid at the livery stables who knew I was setting out to follow you. Won't take long for someone to come out when my horse gets back there without me.'

Despite the dryness of his mouth which was making every word an effort Travis tried hard to maintain a tone of unruffled confidence as he planted the seeds of uncertainty in the minds of his two captors. He glanced briefly beyond them through the trees hoping against hope that Blade wouldn't spoil his argument by suddenly trotting up in search of attention. He and Blade had been partners for over two years, and Travis knew that however spooked the horse might have been by the gunfire he was most unlikely to have gone galloping back to Virginia Springs. Left to his own devices he would more likely have wandered off to forage at a discreet distance until Travis whistled for him.

Brodie's lip curled in disbelief. 'We only got your say-so for that, mister.' He nodded towards his partner. 'Come on, Jeff, let him have it. He's jest stringing us along.'

'And of course,' mused Travis, as if his life weren't hanging on the slenderest of threads, 'I just knew where to follow you without talking to the kid at the livery stables first.'

As he made this remark he stared fully into the eyes trained on him behind the rifle. A momentary furrowing of Booker's eyebrows told him that his point had registered. There was a pause followed by a perceptible relaxing of Booker's trigger finger.

'OK, Travis, you just won yourself a breathing-space.'

'Hey,' protested Brodie, 'You ain't gonna let him walk out of here, Jeff. He'll have the whole town on our heels – it'll ruin everything.'

'Shut your goddarn mouth, bonehead,' snarled Booker. 'You talk plenty, but you ain't no great shakes at thinking. Seems to me that a bullet in the head isn't the only way of disposing of a nosy lawman. Kind of crude, when you think about it. What *sir* here needs is a nice little accident. Somethin' like a broken neck, so nobody'll know how he came by it. That'll keep the heat off us.'

Brodie chuckled in anticipation. 'Yeah, that'd be really sweet. And he'd have to wait for it too. I'll enjoy watching him sweat.'

Booker's mouth curled in a sneer. 'Seems to me he's doing enough of that already.'

Travis flushed, aware of the truth of Booker's jibe. Rivulets of sweat were trickling in all directions down his face.

'Look,' he managed to gasp out, 'I'll cut a deal with you. You let me go and I'll call the matter quits. It'll take me best part of the afternoon to walk back to town. By that time you can be well out of my jurisdiction.'

Booker stared at him for a moment and then shook his head.

'Sorry, Mr Lawman, but that just don't appeal.'

'Why not?'

'Because we don't intend to . . . to . . .'

'Go on, Jeff,' urged Brodie, 'tell the lying rattlesnake what we're . . .'

'Shut up, will you, for chris'sake,' yelled Booker. He turned to Travis again and resumed his sentence. '. . . because we don't intend to incur nobody's attention – and in my experience you can't trust any lawman not to get his cronies together if he gets the chance.'

'So . . .'

'So turn around, Travis. We done enough talking.'

Booker gestured with the rifle.

'Can I put my hands down?' asked Travis as he complied with this order. 'You know I'm not armed.'

'Sure,' said Booker. 'And you can git yourself flat on the ground. Wouldn't want to overtire you.'

As he said this he planted his boot none too gently in Travis's posterior, sending him stumbling forward to fall face down among the ferns.

'Fetch some rope, Pete. Don't think we can allow Mr Travis the use of his hands.'

With his face lodged in the dirt Travis was unable to see where his captors' horses had been concealed, but there was a perceptible interval before he heard Brodie's footsteps returning accompanied by the soft crunch of hoofs on the gravel. Even though some of the soil had stuck in his mouth as he hit the ground the respite from confrontation was a welcome opportunity for him to marshal his thoughts.

Clearly his instinct to follow the two men had been correct, even if he hadn't prepared himself properly. On the other hand, Booker's denial of responsibility for Joel's murder had rung true – and it was the suspicion of their complicity that had set him after them in the first place. But something was clearly planned – and something in the area of Virginia Springs. Booker had managed not to complete his sentence . . . *we don't intend to* . . . but Travis had no difficulty in completing the unspoken thought . . . *we don't intend to leave the area.* Beyond that, there was no point in surmising – if they were planning to carry him along, he would find out soon enough. His thoughts were finally interrupted as Booker approached and crouched down beside him.

'Fraid I'll have to trouble you for your hands, lawman.'

Travis made no difficulty as Booker drew his hands behind his back and proceeded to truss him securely by the wrists with a length of rope supplied by Brodie from one of the horses' saddles. Then he yelped with pain as Booker grasped a handful of his hair and lifted his head up so as to extract the neckerchief that was wound inside Travis's shirt collar. When the neckerchief had been tightly bound over his eyes as a blindfold Travis was prodded to his feet and led stumbling over to one of the horses. Then he felt himself lifted by the combined efforts of both men to lie face down across the saddle with Booker mounted behind.

'Not very comfortable,' he heard Booker remark from somewhere above his head, 'but then we ain't got far to go. You lead, Pete.'

They set off through the trees with Travis trying desperately to maintain some sense of direction. But beyond the fact that they were heading down towards the trail he really couldn't make much sense of things. He surmised that they could scarcely risk actually using the trail itself with the chance that someone might come along and wonder what they were doing with a bound and blindfolded man slung between them – a conjecture which proved correct judging by the unevenness of the ground they were picking their way along. This was certainly no beaten trail.

The discomfort of his position, the increasing agony of the ropes around his tied wrists and the effects of blind fear at the developments of the afternoon caused him to be overcome by a wave of light-headedness – so that he temporarily lost track of time and space. Only a sudden jolt as he was suddenly hauled off the horse and deposited violently on the ground brought him round to full alertness. As he sprawled face down he heard Booker's voice.

'There you are, partner. Ain't that a real pretty view. Shall we share it with the deputy sheriff?'

Travis became aware of someone crouching beside him. Then a pair of rough hands unfastened his blindfold. Blinking in the strong sunlight Travis took a few seconds to recover his vision. What he saw as the world swam back into focus made his heart lurch. They had regained the line of the railroad, with the track only a handstretch away. But what reduced him to a state of quivering inertia was that he was perched on the edge of a gulch, looking straight down into a drop of more than a hundred feet where the track spanned the gap on a narrow trestle-bridge. Beside him Brodie was chuckling as he levered his boot under Travis's ribs.

'Bet you're wishin' you'd let us put a bullet in your head back there, Mr Deputy Sheriff.'

Chapter Seven

Like most young boys Luke Hastings had been accustomed to suffer from a range of standard nightmares which came round with varying frequency. There was the typical one of being chased by a tiger (in his case usually a mountain lion) and being unable to move your feet; there was also a more sinister one of finding that you had been buried alive. Eventually of course you always woke up in the nick of time to avoid actual suffocation – usually to find that your quilt had worked its way right up over your head. His present situation following Scott's departure over the roof was now beginning to evoke unpleasant recollections of his least favourite dream.

After the train drew to a halt even the limited sounds that had penetrated through the crate to Hastings ceased abruptly. He lay curled in his prison listening intently for any signs of activity in the boxcar and fighting off the impulse either to resume hammering for attention or apply the Bowie knife to extricate himself. Only the fear of making himself appear an apostate in Scott's eyes after their affirmation of partnership prevented him from taking precipitate action to free himself.

At last after what seemed an hour, but was probably no more than five minutes, he heard voices approaching the car, together with what sounded like some sort of wagon being drawn up outside. Moments later hollow thuds penetrating from the floorboards beneath him indicated that someone had climbed inside. Muffled voices showed that there were at least two men, but he could pick up no interchange of conversation as crates were briskly removed outside. Whoever was doing the work had done it many times before and evidently had no need either to give or take orders.

The box in which Hastings was concealed was on the side of the car furthest from the open doors, so it was only after some minutes of shifting and sliding that he detected footsteps right against the sides of the crate. Hastings held his breath as two pairs of hands grasped the corners of the crate, tilted it slightly to test the weight, and then began to manoeuvre it across the floor. Hastings braced himself as best he could against the sides to avoid any shift in balance, but whoever was doing the moving did not seem to notice anything unusual.

As the crate reached the doorway it tilted abruptly and slid, presumably on a set of planks that had been lodged for the purpose between the boxcar and the wagon, until it righted itself with an abrupt jerk on the wagon floor. It must have been the last crate, because almost immediately Hastings heard a muffled command, someone geed up the horses and the wagon started to roll.

The change from the gloom of the boxcar was welcome. The bright sunlight penetrated the thin walls of the crate so effectively that for the first time Hastings could actually make out the grain of the timber. The sensation of being entombed dissipated accordingly but this welcome relief did not last long. After a bumpy ride across what was presumably the rail-yard his surroundings darkened as the wagon rolled into some sort of shed and the loading process was reversed. This time the crates were slid unceremoniously down to the floor and arranged in some sort of order. Hastings endured a momentary fit of panic when the possibility dawned on him that he might end up with crates stacked on top of his own, but when the shifting and manoeuvring came to a stop as far as he could make out there was nothing to prevent his exit as planned.

Hastings waited impatiently until he could hear retreating footsteps and voices fading in the distance. He breathed a sigh of relief – so far he had escaped detection. Scott would be pleased. He was fumbling in his belt to extract the Bowie knife so as to prise himself free when it occurred to him that he actually had acquired no information which would be of the slightest use to his partner. The crates had been unloaded – so what? The whole idea had been to obtain inside information, but so far nobody had obliged him by saying anything of the slightest interest. He chewed his lip in indecision.

On the one hand the crate offered him the ideal situation as an eavesdropper – but only if there was someone to eavesdrop on. But on the other hand, if nobody was intending to do any work on the crates he was wasting his time curled up there like a hibernating possum. At length he decided on a compromise – influenced, he freely admitted to himself, at least partly by the increasing discomfort of his cramped position. He would extract himself from the crate, but not from the shed. With so many boxes lying around concealment shouldn't be difficult – and at least he would rid himself of the sensation of being trapped in a coffin.

Keeping his ears open for the sound of any returning footsteps, Hastings carefully inserted the knife-blade under the lid of the crate and began to lever it upwards. Scott's glib assurance that the nails would give easily proved to be only half true: it wasn't that simple to get any purchase or leverage in almost pitch darkness in a confined area where you could scarcely even crouch properly. With patience and many muffled curses, however, at last he began to make progress, and faint shafts of light began to seep between the lid and the sides of the crate. When the lid had been lifted sufficiently for Hastings to get the haft of the knife into the aperture and gain extra leverage progress came faster, One by one the nails relinquished their grip until he was able to apply his shoulders and lift the entire lid free of the surrounding frame.

Hastings peered cautiously around in all directions. From one side of him there was a source of light possibly coming from a window or an open door, but all he could make out was crates seemingly stacked at random. At some distance he could hear the sound of intermittent hammering. Satisfied that he was alone, he let the lid slide to the floor, stood up and stepped out of the crate. He allowed himself the luxury of a long stretch, and then set about replacing the lid so that the crate looked as normal as possible. This proved less easy than he had anticipated. Firstly, the inadequate light made it difficult to see where to refit the nails, secondly he realized that he could only get them back in position by hammering with his boot – with the risk that the noise would attract unwelcome attention.

He pondered this problem for a few moments and then delighted himself with the realization that he had the means to its solution at hand. Smirking at his sharp thinking he untied his neckerchief, wrapped it round the heel of one his boots and used it to thump the nails back into place, trying to time his blows in rhythm with the hammering that he could hear coming from close by. Thus muffled there was little chance that any sound would penetrate outside.

With the crate restored to innocent-looking normality, Hastings was able to examine his surroundings. There was little of interest to be made out. He was in a large wooden shed or depot. The crates had been stacked at one end, while shelves loaded with what looked like mining equipment and supplies ran round the two side walls. In the far end wall there were a set of double doors reaching to ceiling height, one of which had been left partly open, admitting a few streaks of sunlight. Apart from this there were no windows or other source of illumination. Having first checked that he had a clear line of retreat behind the crates, Hastings edged over to the open door and peered cautiously out. Ahead of him was the rail-yard. The only visible activity centred on the locomotive, which had been detached from the leading passenger-car and was evidently preparing to run round to the other end of the train for the return journey. There was no sign of Scott.

He was pondering what to do next when he heard footsteps approaching along the side of the building. Hastings scuttled back to the rear of the shed and placed himself in a corner at the back, crou ching behind one of the newly delivered crates just as the door was booted fully open to reveal two men silhouetted on the threshold.

'Best get started. Cormack don't like no time-wasting.'

The taller of the two led the way towards the crates and pointed to one of the boxes at random.

'You got the crowbar, Jess. Get the lid off this one, while I do a bit of hunting. There's a coupla boxes of supplies somewhere among this lot. Kinda dumb of Abe to dump them just anyhow.'

'Yeah, but it's McCabe's job to oversee the sorting. Seems kind of funny that he ain't showed up. Never knew him to miss a train before.'

'Got himself drunk down at the Meadows, I shouldn't wonder. Money going to his head, you might say. And while you're pawing over those crates best check the bottoms to make sure they're still looking innocent.'

'Hell, why shouldn't they be? Aren't we the best carpenters around? That's why Cormack picked us. It's been a real sweet job.'

While the checking operation proceeded Hastings began to sweat again as he found himself – literally – in a corner. Fortunately, the man called Jess had started work at the far end of the row of crates – methodically levering the lids off the empty boxes and sliding them towards the rear wall – but it was only a matter of time before he or his unnamed partner reached Hastings' place of concealment. Worse than that, one of the crates, of course, contained McCabe's body. Hastings could anticipate some sharp action when the body was disclosed,,but since he had not seen the crates unloaded he had no means of knowing when that exciting moment would occur. As it transpired, it was the man in search of the supply crates who had the first surprise. Putting his hand on the box in which Hastings had recently been concealed, he examined the various bits of paper stuck on the framework and then called for the crowbar. Jess levered off the lid and they peered inside.

'Thought you said this was a supply box, Clint. Somethin' wrong with your eyesight? Seems kinda empty to me.'

Clint's reply was gruff and his expression was puzzled. 'Ought to be, according to these here notices,' He gestured vaguely towards the paperwork affixed to the crate and then scratched his head. 'Don't make sense to me . . .'

'. . . Unless they stuck everything to the wrong box,' Jess remarked.

'Ain't no use speculating. If McCabe was here as he should be we wouldn't be puzzling. Anyhow, we'll find out soon enough when we've opened everything.'

As the work continued Hastings began to engage his brain in precise computations of how many seconds it would take him to leap for the doors when Clint and Jess finally reached his place of concealment. Neither of them looked particularly sprightly, so he reckoned that with the advantage of surprise he could outrun them easily enough, but the question was, where would he be running to? He had never been to Virginia Springs before and had absolutely no idea of the geography of the area. Unless he could find Scott or scuttle to some place of safety he was going to be pretty defenceless. . . .

The two men were about ten feet away from him, and Jess had just levered the lid off another crate when Hastings' speculations were forced to an abrupt end by a startled yell.

'What in tarnation. . . ? Clint, will ya look at this?'

They stared in bewilderment at the contents of the crate.

'So now we know where McCabe is,' said Jess. 'I think we need some more light, partner. Open up the doors.'

Hastings' brow furrowed. The shed doors were open already, surely. What did Jess mean? He was not left long in doubt. Clint vaulted over the remaining crates to the rear wall just a few feet away from where Hastings was crouching and fumbled with an iron bolt. As Hastings focused his gaze on what Clint was doing he suddenly realized that in the uncertain light he had completely misunderstood the nature of his surroundings. What he had taken to be the solid rear wall of the shed was actually a partition formed by a pair of ceiling-height rolling doors. And as Clint pushed them back, light flooded in from the room on the other side.

But this was no shed. Tall windows on either side illuminated the scene with bright sunshine. Hastings could see an area about twice the length of the shed he was standing in, fitted with machinery of all kinds. A couple of what looked to be small smelting-furnaces were placed in

the centre and in one corner there were tidy stacks of
silver ingots presumably waiting to be shipped out. At the
far end a couple of men were hammering away at a
crucible which accounted for the dull thuds Hastings had
heard when he first got out of his crate. He was obviously
looking at Conglomerated's local silver refinery.

The sight came as a surprise. Hastings was vaguely
aware that you didn't dig silver out of the ground in nice
little ready-made bars, but he had always assumed that the
refining was done at the same site as the mine itself.
Ordinarily he would have been fascinated to examine the
means by which the ore was sifted, purified and transformed into shining blocks, but this was no moment for an
illustrated lesson in industrial processing. Clint had
extracted McCabe's body from the crate and laid it out on
the floor. It took him only a moment to digest the implications of the bloodstains on corpse's shirt and then he
yelled at the men by the furnace.

'Hey, will ya come and look at this? Someone stabbed
McCabe.'

The three men in the refining area looked up in
surprise, registered the body at Clint's feet, and came
running over. The flood of light and the disappearance of
the wall behind Hastings back had left him rooted to the
spot and totally exposed. Before he could summon the
presence of mind to duck around the side of a crate he
had been spotted. One of the men pointed and came
running towards him.

'Hey, Clint – you got company in there.'

As Clint turned towards him Hastings made a desperate
attempt to escape. He vaulted over the crates in order to
make a beeline for the open doors. But Jess, who had
remained in his original position, was too quick for him.
As Hastings stumbled past he lifted a boot to bring him
crashing down on the earth floor. Before he could scram-

ble to his feet Jess had landed a well-aimed kick at his head and for the second time that day Hastings lapsed into semi-consciousness.

It was like a reproduction of another of his boyhood nightmares – the feet that refused to move when you desperately needed to run for safety. Except that this time the mountain lion had really caught him. When he recovered his wits he found that he had been lifted up and frogmarched into the smelting area beside one of the furnaces. Two men were holding him, painfully, with his arms pinioned behind his back, while a third was tilting his chin up so as to let the light fall fully on his face.

'Ain't nothing but a kid. Anyone recognize him?'

Hastings' captors looked at each other blankly, so now the man addressed Hastings directly, thrusting his fist sharply under his chin to emphasize the threat of impending violence.

'OK, kid. Who are you?'

'Hastings, Luke Hastings.'

'Where are you from?'

'Drummond's Crossing.'

Hastings had been wriggling helplessly as he gasped out these two replies, but he was held in an iron grip that was actually stretching his chest muscles and making it difficult to breathe.

'Please, mister. Tell them to let go of me. I'm answering your questions.'

His inquisitor scowled, 'We gotta few more questions yet, kiddo – and you'd better answer them good and quick. How did ya get here?'

'On the train, mister. I . . . I just stowed away for a ride. I ain't never seen Virginia Springs before.'

'That so? Don't reckon you'll be seeing much of it today.'

This remark was accompanied by a general guffaw.

Then the inquisition continued.

'We just discovered that one of our friends arrived here in a box. Dead. I suppose you wouldn't know anything about that, Mr Stowaway.'

'I didn't kill him, mister. I swear.'

From behind Hastings' left ear Jess spoke with a snarl.

'He's a lying little rattlesnake. Why, looky here . . .'

Hastings felt a hand fumbling at his belt as Jess spoke again, brandishing McCabe's Bowie knife in front of his face.

'What's he doin' with McCabe's knife stuck in his belt? Kind of unmistakable with that fancy handle.'

The man facing Hastings took the knife and examined it carefully.

'Seems like Jess is right, kid. You are a lying little skunk. So how did you come by this knife if you didn't take it off McCabe?'

'I . . . it was in the boxcar. I just picked it up.'

'Yeah? And you *just* dumped McCabe in a crate after you *just* stabbed him, and . . .'

'No, mister. You got it wrong. I . . .'

Hastings' protest was cut short by an impatient oath from his inquisitor.

'All right, kid. We ain't got all day to waste with your lies.'

His hand dropped from Hastings' chin. Then he unbuttoned Hastings' shirt and spread it back to display his bare chest.

'There's a quick way to get the whole story without dragging it out of you bit by bit.'

He turned to the furnace where various smelting-tools and crucibles were lying ready for use. After a pause while he wrapped a cloth carefully around his hand he picked up a short metal rod bearing what appeared to be a circular disc at the end – similar in appearance, although not in scale, to a cattle-branding iron. Hastings could see that the disc, which had been resting right at the edge of the flames was glowing nearly red hot.

'This little trinket,' said the man, turning to face Hastings, 'we use for stamping the Company's monogram on the ingots. It produces a real pretty design. Ain't never seen its effect on human skin, but I guess it's equally effective.'

Hastings began to writhe and kick frantically as the iron approached his bare chest and flakes of red hot ash began to sprinkle down, singeing his flesh.

'Please, mister. Don't do it. I told you I ain't no killer. I was just joyriding. . . .'

'Jeez, that's a good one,' chuckled Jess. 'Let him have it real good, Pete. The way he done it to McCabe.'

As he felt the scorching tip of the iron coming towards contact with his skin, Hastings ceased struggling and prepared to tell the whole truth. But before he could open his mouth to surrender a door further along the refinery swung open and two men appeared.

'What in tarnation is going on here?'

The voice carried sufficient authority for Pete to lower the iron before any further damage was inflicted on Hastings' chest. He turned to address the newcomer.

'We got trouble, chief. Jess and Clint found McCabe in a crate, stabbed. Then we find this kid in here with McCabe's knife.'

The chief, a silver-haired man neatly attired with jacket and vest despite the heat, approached the frozen tableau around the furnace. He frowned.

'McCabe dead?'

'Sure thing.' Pete gestured towards the sprawled body. 'We found him in a crate. Then we found this little rattlesnake skulking around the boxes with McCabe's knife stuck in his belt.'

The chief stared at Hastings' dishevelled figure. He was still pinioned by the arms, but had temporarily stopped thrashing about. His shirt was still wide open to reveal a chest spattered with red blotches and blisters where the sparks from the iron had settled on his skin.

'Seems like you owe somebody an explanation, young man.'

'Sure does,' said Pete, before Hastings had a chance to open his mouth. 'That's what we was trying to extract when you came in.'

The pressure on Hastings' arms had relaxed a little, and Pete, although still holding the iron, had stopped brandishing it. As his terror receded, and Hastings felt able to take his eyes off the instrument of retribution, he found himself staring across at a familiar figure. The second man who had entered was Scott. As a wave of relief swept over him Hastings attempted to point, forgetting that he was still held by the arms.

'He . . . he can tell ya. . . .'

'About what?' Scott had approached but was offering no sign of recognition. 'I've never set eyes on him.'

'Hey, wait a minute,' Hastings yelled, 'we rode up together.'

Scott stared round at the others. 'Did anyone see him get off the passenger car with me?'

There was no reply. 'Look, what is this?' Hastings had started to struggle again. 'He can tell ya . . .'

'I think,' said the chief, cutting in sharply, 'that we need to stop wasting time. We've got a dead man here and somebody killed him.'

'Right,' agreed Pete, resuming his stance with the iron. Scott raised a warning finger. 'But not precipitately, surely. There's the Company's reputation to consider. Out East, I don't think the railroads use molten metal to deal with stowaways. I believe a billy-club applied with sufficient vigour to arms and legs is usually reckoned sufficient – or failing that, a pick-axe handle . . .'

'Hey,' yelled Hastings, 'You can't . . .'

'No problem,' remarked the chief. 'We aren't exactly short of suitable lengths of timber around here.'

'But . . .'

Hastings' voice trailed away as his legs turned to jelly and his captors let him slide to the floor. Scott bent down to examine his face and then straightened up with a slight smile.

'Why, Mr Cormack, I do believe he's fainted.'

Chapter Eight

Nick Travis would never have described himself as a religious man, but as Brodie's boot levered away under his ribs and he found himself staring down into certain death, his thoughts turned for a second to the Almighty with the unframed question *why him and why like this?* But before the seemingly inevitable could happen he heard Booker's voice.

'Jesus, what kind of dumb coyote are you, Brodie?'

The pressure under Travis's ribs eased slightly.

'Huh? This is where we pitch him over, right?'

'Sure. It'll make a real nice suicide. Dead man at the bottom of a gulch *with his hands tied behind his back.* Real convincing.'

'Oh. Well, ain't no problem fixing that. I'll get a knife.'

As Brodie's footsteps retreated across the gravel towards the horses, Travis twisted his head round to face Booker.

'You really going through with this? Nobody's going to believe that I just fell off a cliff without a bit of assistance. Sooner or later they'll pin it on you.'

'Yeah? That's a chance we'll have to take. We got a train to stop, Travis. And you're in the way. A thousand bucks apiece should see us well clear of trouble.'

'If you get it – but it didn't go that easy for you down in Flagstaff, did it?'

'So you do know who we are, then?'

'I didn't when I first saw you back in the saloon. But since then I've had time to search my memory. Then I recalled that I'd seen your faces on some old Wanted posters in the sheriff's office. I also recollect that you both got a year in the Arizona penitentiary when they caught up with you.'

By now Brodie had returned with a knife which he handed to Booker.

'Ain't this nice, Pete? Deputy sheriff knows all about our little problem after the train job down in Flagstaff. Seems concerned that this afternoon's little enterprise ain't going to turn a profit for us.'

'Yeah?' said Brodie, unable to resist the opportunity to plant his boot into Travis's chest. 'Well, did ya tell Mr Smartpants Travis that we've already been paid. This ain't no . . .'

'Cut it out, partner. We don't want to bore him with details.'

Booker knelt down and began to hack the knots loose from the rope that bound Travis's wrists. The precious few seconds of conversation had given Travis the opportunity to take brief stock of his situation. With certain death behind his head, there was nothing to be lost by a final effort to save himself As the rope fell away and his wrists came free, Travis seized his opportunity.

'You forgot my guns Booker – I wouldn't be diving off a cliff without them.'

Booker grunted in sudden perplexity at being reminded of this glaring omission in the suicide scenario and made the mistake of fractionally taking his eye off his victim. Before Booker could stand up Travis gathered his strength and aimed a sideswipe at his chin. Delivered from a horizontal position the punch was inexact and delivered at only half force, but it was enough to pitch Booker backwards into Brodie's boots.

With both of them momentarily unbalanced Travis rolled himself upright and launched himself away from the cliff edge. As Brodie had been fetching the knife Travis had seen that both horses were tethered, so they offered no hope of escape even if he had been able to mount one without getting shot. But even so, they provided the means of salvation. As the two cursing gunmen righted themselves and reached for their pistols Travis dived under the horses' hoofs, rolled himself right under the startled animals and scuttled into the undergrowth beyond. By preventing Brodie and Booker from firing into his retreating back the horses had provided him with just enough temporary cover to have some chance of escape. It was true that two men on horses ought to have no trouble hunting down an unarmed man with no mount at his disposal. But Travis knew where he was, and was familiar with every inch of the terrain between the bridge and town – he'd quartered it often enough with Blade in the course of his duties.

So now, as the two gunmen wasted more precious seconds untethering and mounting their horses, Travis ran ducking and weaving between rocks and trees, picking the most difficult route for horses to follow but steadily manoeuvring himself in a direction that led back to the trail and Virginia Springs. It was less than half a minute before the first shot whistled over his head followed by a second which nicked the flesh in his upper arm. Travis yelled with the shock. Then, momentarily distracted by the sudden pain he tripped over a root, fell sprawling and then found himself rolling down over rocks and shrubs into a steep, narrow gully. Brought to a sudden painful stop by a boulder which impeded his downward momentum, Travis heard the two riders approach and halt some way above him.

'You get him?' he heard Brodie ask.

'Sure. Didn't ya hear him yell?'

'Then where in tarnation is he?'

'Down the bottom of the gully of course.'

'Do you reckon we should go down and make sure of him.'

Booker's voice was scornful. 'If you feel like winding your horse down there and up again you're welcome. Even if he's only winged he aint getting back to town without a horse. Come on, we haven't got time to waste.'

Travis waited until the hoofs had retreated, then he cautiously stood up. Forgetting that the heel of one of his boots had been partly shot away he lost his balance on the precipitous ground and found himself rolling downwards again. Despite the pain Travis did nothing to arrest his fall. When he finally fetched up at the bottom beside one of the many rills that trickled off higher ground in these parts his pursuers were out of sight.

He was just wondering whether to follow the stream downhill or cross it and try to lose himself in the undergrowth beyond, when his prospects changed dramatically. There, not fifty yards away, was Blade drinking placidly, having presumably followed Travis's entire abduction at a discreet distance and having enjoyed an hour's unlimited foraging in the process. As Travis whistled softly the horse pricked up his ears, stopped drinking, and stared in Travis's direction. Then he lowered his head and resumed drinking.

'You bastard horse, get over here.' The urge to yell at the animal was all but irresistible but Travis couldn't risk revealing his position to the men up above in case they should look back – so the enforced mumble served purely to release his own anxiety. He whistled again. This time Blade looked at him and came trotting down as nonchalantly as if they had been out on a Sunday afternoon joyride.

'About time, you idle critter,' remarked Travis affectionately, as he scanned the treeline above, slid crouching on to the horse's back and spurred him hell for leather down the watercourse. As Travis manoeuvred the horse back towards the main trail, he knew he was safe. But of course the afternoon's business was scarcely begun. When they finally hit the road Travis dug in his heels and set Blade into a gallop that he intended to maintain until they reached town. The horse had just enjoyed an easy hour. Now he could do some hard work. . . .

Another of Luke Hastings' least favourite nightmares had returned to haunt him. This time he was drowning. Arms and legs thrashing wildly proved useless against the waves that were engulfing him. He was choking helplessly and about to go under when he made one last effort to open his eyes. Blinking in the bright sunlight he attempted to raise his head – and then fell back as a real bout of coughing and spluttering overcame him. Turning on his side he spat out what felt like a gallon of cold water. When the choking spasm had passed he opened his eyes again to take stock of his situation.

He was stretched on a wooden bench and his head and shoulders had been dowsed with cold water. Just a yard or so away from his nose a grille of iron bars stretched from floor to ceiling. Beyond it a grey-haired figure with a silver star pinned above his vest pocket was standing holding an empty wooden bucket whose contents presumably had just been released over Hastings' recumbent torso.

'Thought that'd get you going. Never fails.'

Hastings sat up, wiping the residue of water from his eyes. Then a wave of anger overtook him.

'Hey mister. You just ruined my shirt. It was clean on this morning.'

'Yeah? Could have fooled me. Looked as though you spent the night in it.'

Hastings stood up, approached the grille and rattled the bars impotently.

'You gonna let me out of here?'

Putting down the bucket, the grey-haired figure studied him for a moment.

'Don't see any immediate prospect of that, youngster – seeing as you're under arrest.'

'Under arrest? What in tarnation for?'

'Murder, of course. That's what we usually call it in these parts when you stick a knife in somebody without his permission.'

Hastings reeled momentarily and staggered back to the bench to sit down and collect his thoughts. The dowsing of cold water had brought him back to consciousness so abruptly that the events of the morning had been mentally wiped out. Now they started to seep back. He could remember the train, a dead body, the crates, the hot iron, something about billy-clubs and someone called Scott. In an access of panic Hastings stood up again and clutched desperately at the iron grille.

'Mister, I ain't done nothing. I'm innocent. It was. . . .'

He paused as another voice from behind the sheriff cut into the conversation. 'My, he sure does like shooting his mouth off, doesn't he?'

The voice was disturbingly familiar. Hastings craned his neck to see past the sheriff who was partly blocking his view of the rest of the room. Beyond he could make out a small office furnished with a desk and swivel-chair occupied by a man with his back to the cell. As Hastings stared, he swivelled round and stretched himself out with his hands behind his head like an old-timer on a stoop at sunset with the prospect of an evening ahead doing sweet nothing. Hastings yelled across at him.

'Scott, you skunk. Get me outta here, will you?'

The sheriff sighed and waved an admonitory finger.

'Hey, youngster, that ain't no way to talk to Mr Truscott – specially after he saved you from a possible lynching. Some of those guys down at the depot aren't too pleased about what you did to their buddy.'

'I didn't do nothing. You ask *him* what happened. . . .' Hastings jabbed his finger frantically in Scott's (or was it Truscott's?) direction.

'I already heard.' The sheriff's curt tone suggested that he was in no mood to spend time listening to any protests from Hastings. 'They find McCabe rolled up in a box. stabbed, and they find you in there with him and his knife tucked in your belt. Seems, if you'll pardon the jest, like an open and shut case to me.'

'Well, it ain't. And Scott knows why. Look, I got rights. I want a lawyer.'

With a dry chuckle the sheriff turned towards the figure stretched out at the desk.

'Did ya hear that? He wants a lawyer. Son,' he said, turning back to Hastings, 'I'm the only law*man* you're likely to see, here, so make the best of me and don't tax my patience. As I was saying, according to Mr Truscott here, they were fixing to give you a real good working-over when he managed to persuade the depot manager to put you in my charge. This is the safest place for you till emotions cool down a bit and we can arrange to get you hanged legally.'

'For something I didn't do? You listen good, Sheriff, and I'll tell you exactly . . .'

But before Hastings could say any more there was a thumping of boots on the boardwalk outside the office. The door burst open and one of the local livery stable urchins thrust his head in.

'Hey, Sheriff, Mr Travis sent me to find you. He's down at Doc Maguire's . . .'

'Doc. . . ?'

'Yeah. Seems like someone's taken a shot at him.'

'OK.' The sheriff turned to his two guests. 'Looks as though my deputy may have run into a little trouble. If you'll excuse me gentlemen, I'll be right back. Doc's surgery's only a block away.'

Having ostentatiously pocketed the keys to the lock-up, the sheriff collected his hat and prepared to follow the urchin outside. 'I'll leave the boy in your company, Mr Truscott. Call me if a lynch mob looks like gathering.'

As the office door closed, leaving Hastings alone with his erstwhile colleague, Scott's demeanour changed dramatically. He sprang out of the chair and strode over to the bars.

'Well done, partner. That fainting routine was the best bit of acting I've seen west of Chicago. It had them all fooled.'

Hastings scowled. 'What acting? I really did pass out. So would you if you'd just been near branded. And I ain't your partner. After what you've landed me in, our partnership's dissolved.'

'Yeah? Takes two to make a partnership – and two to break it. I'd think about it carefully if I were you. Remember *you still need me* – I'm the only one who knows the truth. And I'm not about to incriminate myself yet.'

Hastings took a moment to digest the implications of what he had just heard. Then he jutted his head aggressively towards the other man.

'OK, you low-down coyote, but you remember that you need me as much as I need you. I got some real information while I was stashed away in that shed. If you want it we gotta set ourselves on a proper footing. And that means you putting yourself on the level with me. You didn't even tell me the truth about your name. Is it really Truscott?'

'Yes, it is. And I didn't lie to you. I told you to *call* me Scott

– I didn't say it was my real name.'

'And how come you was threatening to have me whacked with billy-clubs – or was it pick-axe handles – in that depot? Didn't sound very partner-like. . . .'

'Better than watching the company's monogram being burnt into your chest – which is what was about to happen when I walked in, if I remember correctly. I was buying time, you dummy.'

Truscott's tone had become both reassuring and encouraging.

'Look, Hastings – Luke – sit down on that bench and I'll tell you what happened. Then you can tell me what you found out – if you feel like it.'

Hastings stared at him, decided that there was no point in continuing the argument standing up, and sat down, his expression still sullen, on the damp bench.

'That's more like it,' said Truscott. 'OK. So the train pulls into Virginia Springs and I step off. First surprise is that nobody's waiting for me. I wait a bit and then two guys roll up with a wagon so I ask them where the depot manager is. Turns out to be that guy Cormack who you saw down by the furnace. I find him in his office which is round the back of the shed where they store the crates. He seems surprised that I've turned up, and I'm surprised that he's surprised and wasn't expecting me – considering that I wired earlier this morning, as I told you. So that's three surprises. Next thing I discover is that the railroad dispatcher-cum-telegraph operator was found stabbed early this morning. That's another surprise, but it explains why Cormack never got my message. I think.'

Hastings' sullen expression had transformed itself into one of rapt attention as Truscott spoke. Now he permitted himself a whistle of real interest.

'Wow. Seems like there's been an awful lot of stabbing goin' on today.'

'Right, anyway, first thing Cormack wants to know is why McCabe wasn't on the train with me. I say I haven't seen him since Truckee Meadows and thought he was in the boxcar. Cormack hasn't got any way of knowing the truth of that because apparently the telegraph man was the only one they've got here. Nobody else can read the incoming messages, or tap any out. He's completely in the dark.'

'Kind of convenient.'

'Exactly. So then I tell him I'm here to check on some of the local paperwork, without revealing exactly what I've already found out. We chew the cud a bit, and he's just pointing me in the direction of the mine when I hear your voice yelling through the wall. So we come to investigate. Naturally while I'm standing there I'm afraid you're going to shoot your mouth off about me. I was all ready to sock you another one on the jaw when you obliged me by passing out. I thought it was real good timing. Then I persuaded Cormack that maybe it would be better to keep things legal and hand you over to the sheriff. So we brought you up here.'

'You're right about the timing. I sure was ready to spill the beans. I ain't that much of a hero.'

'Right. So that's my story. What's yours?'

Hastings took a moment to consider. It was clear enough that it was his information rather than his person that was of value to Truscott. Once he had revealed what he knew, there was nothing to stop the other man walking out and leaving him to his fate. His doubts must have been written all over his features, because it was Truscott who spoke next.

'You're scared I'll leave you in the lurch as soon as you've told me what you know.'

Hastings nodded. 'Something like that.'

Truscott sighed, reached in his pants pocket and

extracted a leather billfold. From one of the pockets he produced a folded slip of paper which he proffered through the bars to Hastings.

'Read it.'

Hastings leant forward, took the paper and read it. It was a note of credence under the letterhead and seal of the Conglomerated Mining Company certifying the bearer's status as a bona fide agent.

'OK,' said Hastings, 'so it proves you're who you say you are. Still doesn't prove you'll get me off the hook.' He handed the letter back, but Truscott declined to take it.

'Keep it for the moment if you don't trust me, Considering that we're supposed never to have met before it'll buttress your story if you ever have to talk your way out.'

There was a long silence as Hastings considered what to do. Then he folded up the letter and stuffed it in his shirt pocket. He grinned at Truscott.

'Cormack's your man. And them other two who was holding me when you walked in.' Hastings proceeded to relate what he had overheard in the shed. Truscott exhaled audibly.

'It all links up,' he said, when Hastings had finished. 'McCabe as the guard was the linkman between here and the other end of the line. The two depot men do the packing – legal and illegal – and Cormack fixes the paperwork.'

'And he killed the dispatcher, too,' interjected Hastings in growing excitement.

'How do you reckon that?'

'When he got your message this morning he panicked and fixed things so there would be no more messages in or out. Gave himself time to work out how much of a danger you really were. Easy enough for him to lie to you about not receiving it.'

Truscott rubbed his chin thoughtfully.

'It certainly fits – although I wouldn't have reckoned Cormack as a knifeman. In any case . . .'

Truscott's ruminations were interrupted by footsteps returning along the boardwalk. The sheriff entered the office accompanied by a tall young man wearing a silver star on his vest which was slightly stained with blood that had obviously seeped ftom his shirt-sleeve. The sheriff made a brief introduction.

'Travis, this is Mr Truscott, sent out from Chicago by CMC. We had a spot of bother here.' He indicated Hastings, skulking in the cell. 'Seems like junior here did for Jed McCabe. He arrived up from the Meadows dead.'

Travis shook hands with Truscott and sat wearily down in the swivel-chair, massaging his arm.

'Looks like you've had a bit of bother of your own, Mr Travis.' said Truscott. 'Are you all right?'

Travis nodded. 'Bullet took a sliver out of my arm. Bled a bit but Doc's splashed physic all over it and bandaged it up. I'll live.' He stared at Truscott. 'We seem to have trouble all round – and it concerns the Company. Is your appearance here entirely coincidental?'

'Maybe, maybe not.'

Truscott studied the sheriff and his deputy in turn.

'Look, can I tell you something in confidence?'

'I think you'd better.' Travis's reply was immediate.

'There's a matter of some missing silver which my employers aren't too happy about. That's why I'm here.'

'Very timely,' remarked Travis. 'Because if my experience this morning means anything, I think you're about to miss quite a bit more. I was bushwhacked by two characters who seem intent on relieving you of the next train-load.'

Truscott shook his head.

'Maybe, but not immediately, I think. I sent instructions

this morning to hold any further consignments. Except
... my God ... I'd forgotten ...' Truscott clutched his
head in irritation. 'Cormack claimed he never received
the wire. So the train ...'

He rushed to the door and strode out on to the boardwalk from where there was a clear view down the street to
the depot and the railhead. The train had pulled out.

Chapter Nine

Truscott turned back into the sheriff's office with an expression of extreme self-reproach on his face.

'Looks like I've lost the train and a consignment of silver. Can we get up a posse? If we act quick enough there may still be a chance of recovering something.'

The two lawmen exchanged wry glances. Then Travis burst out laughing.

'Mister, this is Virginia Springs, not Dodge City. Do you reckon me or the sheriff can just walk outside and summon a bunch of good men and true to saddle up at a moment's notice? This is a working township and we don't have any surplus hands just itching to turn themselves into heroes. Try deputizing anyone in this town and they're likely to turn round and ask what the appointed law officers think they're paid for.'

Truscott rubbed his jaw. 'Good point, Travis. But of course, that's partly the issue, isn't it?'

'What do you mean?'

'It's a question of what you're paid for.'

'Hey, now look here . . .'

'Easy, easy,' said Truscott as Travis stood up and moved threateningly towards him. 'Don't take it personal. All I was trying to say is that you and I work for the same employer – CMC, right? I even know how much the company pays for your services. So when the chips are down the company has certain calls on your time and attention. Seems to me we're in the middle of some sort of conspiracy here and I'm not leaving till it's sorted out. Posse or no posse, I at least need to know *you're* as committed as I am.'

Travis gestured angrily towards his injured left arm.

'See that, Truscott? That's the extent of my commitment already. You got any similar battle scars to parade?'

Truscott smiled.

'No, but I've notched up one scalp in the company's service today.'

'Yeah? Like who?'

'McCabe.'

There was a startled oath from Turner as he stared at Truscott with fists tightly clenched. Then he glanced back at the cell where Hastings was still sprawled on the bench.

'McCabe? But I thought . . . I mean . . . we've got the kid locked up for that.'

'Sure, but like he said, he didn't do it. And before either of you treats this as a confession of murder and puts me behind bars, let me make it clear that it was self-defence. McCabe jumped me, there was a scuffle and I let him have it with his own knife. Later I passed it to Hastings for other purposes. That's how they found him with it.'

'Now, wait a minute,' protested Turner, his face red with anger and bewilderment, 'you're leaving me way behind on this one, mister. You mean you've been stringing us all along? We've only got your word for all of this. Meanwhile I've got two dead bodies on my hands. Seems to me I should lock you up with the kid until we can get this properly sorted out.'

'I don't think it would advance your cause, Sheriff.' Truscott smiled emolliently. 'And I don't think CMC

would take too kindly to knowing that you locked up two
of their representatives.'

Turner uttered a snort of contempt. 'Yeah, well they
can . . .' Turner cut off his own sentence as he registered
the full import of what Truscott had just said. 'Two?
But . . .'

'That's right,' said Truscott gesturing towards the
disconsolate figure in the cell. 'He works for CMC too.'
Truscott then raised his voice a little, speaking to Hastings.
'Isn't that right, Mr Hastings?'

Hastings, who had never heard himself addressed as *Mr*
before, glanced around in bemusement as if there were
someone else with him in the cell. Then he stood up and
walked to the bars. 'Huh? Oh, . . . er . . . sure.'

Turner shook his head in disbelief 'This is all bullshit,
and I've a mind to lock you up for wasting my time.'

Ignoring the sheriff's threat, Truscott turned towards
Travis, who had been following the previous interchange
in silence but with close attention.

'Mr Hastings has credentials which you can easily verify.
Would you care to do so?'

Travis nodded. 'All right.'

Truscott stared expectantly across at Hastings who
stood rooted and immobile. Then, as Travis came up to
the bars, Hastings recollected himself. Trying to control
the trembling of his hand he reached into his shirt pocket,
extracted a folded piece of paper and handed it through
the bars to Travis. Repressing the wave of panic which had
nearly engulfed him over the last ten minutes he tried to
keep his voice as even and businesslike as Truscott's. In a
passable imitation of the tones of a lawyer from east of the
Mississippi he heard himself say, 'This should settle the
matter to your satisfaction.'

Travis unfolded the paper, read it, and handed it back
to Hastings without comment. He frowned. After a long

pause during which nobody in the room seemed to breathe, he turned to the sheriff.

'Let him out.'

'Are you crazy, Travis?' There was a note of panic in Turner's protest. 'Two corpses in the morgue and you want us to end up with an empty cell?'

Travis stepped across with his right hand outstretched. 'Gimme the keys. I'll take responsibility.'

'The hell you will, mister. You may be on the company payroll, but I'm still the sheriff here.'

'Sure you are. I said let him out. I didn't I say let him go. He's a company man and I'll take him into my own custody till all this is settled. Anything goes wrong you can have my hide.'

'You bet your bottom dollar I will, Nick. You're way out of line on this.'

The two men eyeballed each other, but Travis's stare was unwavering. After a long minute Turner reached in his pocket and produced the keys. He tossed them contemptuously to his deputy.

'Take 'em, then – and let him out yourself. Like you said, it's your responsibility.'

Travis unlocked the door. He grasped Hastings by the shoulder establishing an eye contact that contrived to be both threatening and complicit.

'Like I just said to the sheriff I'm letting you out, but you're still in my custody. You make one move without my permission and I'll gun you down. Understood?'

'Understood.'

Truscott nodded with satisfaction as Hastings stepped out of the cell.

'Now can we get down to business? I've got a consignment to check.'

'Easy does it, mister.' Turner's tone was still truculent. 'I still give the orders round here, company or no company.

You ain't lost your train.'

'But . . .'

'But nothin'. They've hauled it along to the woodstack, which for reasons best known to the railroad is along towards the north edge of town. Unless they're proposing to run on air it'll take a while to replenish the tender.'

Truscott heaved a sigh of relief.

'Let's go, then.'

'Sure,' said Turner, his voice heavy with sarcasm. 'You got a horse?'

'It seems to me,' said Travis, 'that we're in danger of going about things without due preparation. I made that mistake myself this morning and I nearly got myself killed.'

'Go on,' said Truscott.

'Well, there's four of us, so that's not bad as far as manpower's concerned. But as the sheriff says, there's two of you without horses – something of a disadvantage in this part of the world.'

'OK. So we hire them.'

'Right. Then there's the question of firepower.' Travis gestured down at his naked hips. 'Seems like there's three of us without so much as a peashooter between us.'

Turner stared at the empty holsters. 'What in tarnation. . . ?'

'The two gentlemen I told you about relieved me of them this morning and omitted to return them. And that reminds me . . .'

Travis walked over to a small bureau that stood by one wall and began to rummage through the drawers.

'Hey,' protested Turner, 'what the heck . . .'

'OK, OK,' said Travis as his thumb lighted on the sheet of paper he had been looking for. He held up a yellowing Wanted notice, displaying the unkempt faces of Brodie and Booker. 'Just wanted to make sure that I'd got things right, These are the two that jumped me. Kind of lucky this bit of paper was still lying about.'

'Yeah,' said Turner, 'well, you got yourself to thank, then. It's the deputy's job to take care of the filing.'

Truscott made a gesture of impatience. 'Fine, so we know who we're looking for. Now can we get on with the job of finding them. . . ?'

'Sure,' said Travis. 'But I got one small but important technical detail to attend to, if you don't mind.' He turned his attention to a cabinet which stood alongside the bureau. Using a key from the same bunch that had procured Hastings' freedom he opened it up to reveal an assortment of weaponry and gunbelts presumably confiscated from the local citizenry or passing travellers, and never returned. Having made a careful selection, Travis accoutred himself with a pair of Colts which he proceeded to load. Truscott, who had been visibly chafing while Travis took his time, made impatiently for the door.

'Perhaps we can . . .'

'Just hold it a minute, mister,' said Turner, who had been watching Travis's activity in silence. 'You going to parade junior here down the boardwalk?'

'Hey,' protested Hastings, 'I ain't no . . .'

'Because I ought to remind you that he's just liable to get himself lynched. That's the reason you brung him up here in the first place.'

'Sheriff's right,' said Travis. 'We need a coupla horses first.'

'See to it, Nick, for chrissake,' said Turner, with a trace of weariness in his voice. 'I'll go and make sure the train don't move – at least until its scheduled to.'

Truscott looked puzzled. 'Why can't you just stop it, *period?*'

'Because I ain't got no jurisdiction over the railroad operations.'

'No, but there must be someone here who has.'

Turner's lips opened with a sneer.

'Sure. His name's Joel Bentham and he's lying flat out in the morgue. You any good at resuscitation?'

Without waiting for a reply Turner spun on his heel and walked out of the office, slamming the door behind him.

'Right,' said Travis, walking round behind Hastings, 'so let's get down to business. Now which of you coyotes is going to tell me what's really been going on?'

'Hey,' protested Hastings, 'we just . . .'

But the muzzle of the Colt with which Travis had just rearmed himself was now pressing into his neck. Hastings gulped and stared helplessly at Truscott, hoping for some sort of inspiration.

'I'm willing to believe,' said Travis, 'that one of you is working for CMC; but not both. What kind of a hayseed do you take me for? I want an explanation, and I want it quick, otherwise I'll blow kiddo's brains out and call it *shot while trying to evade custody.*'

Truscott spoke. 'Put the gun down, Travis. You're right of course. But I think we're all on the same side. This is what's happened. . . .'

Travis didn't put the gun down immediately, but Hastings found the pressure on his neck gradually easing as Truscott gave a truthful account of the morning's events. When he had finished, Travis put the gun back in its holster and sat down at the desk.

'OK. Now I'll tell you what happened to me this morning and we'll see if we can put two and two together and make it add up to four. At the moment all I'm getting is fractions.'

When the pooling of information was complete Truscott rose from his chair to stare contemplatively out of the window.

'Seems to me,' he said, turning to face the other two,

'that we have to decide whether we're confronting two plots or one.'

'But it's straightforward, isn't it?' Hastings shrugged. 'You got Cormack and cronies defrauding the company by under-delivering silver. You even know how they've been doing it – including how Cormack killed that telegraph man to cut communications. That's one scheme. Then Travis here hits on two bandidos planning a train hold-up the way they've done it before. That's' another plot. Just coincidence that they're happening at the same time.'

'It's the coincidence that's worrying me,' said Travis. 'And Cormack didn't kill Joel Bentham, by the way. When I walked over to the depot first thing this morning Cormack was in the Parlour having breakfast with some of his men. He couldn't have done it unless he's got wings under his vest.'

Unabashed by the demolition of his solution to Bentham's murder Hastings persisted. 'OK, so someone else did it. But it doesn't mean there's any connection between Cormack and your two men.'

'Agreed. Booker and Brodie are two run of the mill no-goods who go from one unsuccessful robbery to another until they get shut up in the state pen for keeps. On the face of it stopping a silver-train looks like another typical job. Except ... if I understood them correctly, they've already been paid for it.'

'And if they've been paid for it up front,' said Truscott, continuing the argument, 'there's a third party behind it. And someone with ready cash, too.'

'Quite a bit of ready cash,' said Travis.

'OK, OK,' said Hastings, 'It still don't connect them with Cormack and friends. If they're busy helping themselves to silver without being caught, why would they want to pay someone, to rob their own train? Don't make any kind of sense.'

'Yes,' agreed Travis. 'It's a weak point in the argument. But there must be an explanation.'

'Anyway,' intervened Truscott, snapping his fingers with impatience, 'it really doesn't matter. If we hold the train there isn't going to be any robbery. Let's concentrate on cleaning up here. I've already got enough evidence for you to make some arrests even if we don't know who killed Bentham. Put a few people behind bars and someone's sure to start squealing to save their own skin. You'll get your murderer in the end. So let's get started.'

Travis made no move. Instead, he shook his head slowly.

'Fraid I ain't inclined to rush into anything yet, Truscott. I can't see the whole picture.'

'But I just said . . .'

'I heard what you said. But what's the hurry? Cormack isn't going anywhere – and if he does we can pick him up easy enough. I'm inclined to let things develop a bit further. It'll kind of give people time to declare themselves, if you know what I mean.'

'Yeah,' said Truscott with a distinct note of hostility in his voice. 'I think I get your drift. And I don't like it. It means . . .'

'It means I want to let the train go. Before we make any arrests here. Got it in one, mister.'

'Hey,' protested Hastings. 'Booker and Brodie are your problem. Truscott and I done our bit. I wanna get back to my ranch.'

Travis smiled. 'Of course you do. And I'm quite ready to oblige you.'

Hastings relaxed visibly. 'Glad to hear it.'

'It seems to me,' continued Travis, 'that considering the distance, it'll be quickest by train. It's also the neatest way of getting you out of the way of the local lynch mob.'

'Oh sure,' said Hastings, his eyes narrowing in suspicion as he tried to second guess what Travis was leading up to. 'And I suppose I just mosey up with a ticket and pitch myself in the passenger car. Bit public, ain't it?'

'A bit. But I was intending you to ride in the boxcar. After all, that's the way you came up, isn't it?'

Hastings stared at the deputy sheriff, his face a mixture of disbelief and rising anger. Then he turned to Truscott.

'Oh, I get it. He wants to turn me into some sort of . . . So when the shooting starts I'll be on the inside.'

'He's sharp, ain't he?' Travis smiled across at Truscott.

'You bet. That's why I picked him. It's that guileless face – makes him a born agent.'

As the conversation seemed set to continue over his head, Hastings raised his voice in protest. 'Hey, wait a minute, wait a minute. I'm still in the room, aren't I? Seems to me I've got a say in all this.'

'Sure you have,' said Travis equably. 'You can either agree or go back in that cell. Remember, you're still in custody.'

'You gonna let him do this to me, Truscott? This is all your making. If you hadn't bazooka'd me back there at Drummond's none of this would have happened.'

'Don't think I've got much choice. As long as you're in custody you're effectively Mr Travis's property. Can't say as I like it . . . but there is the possible lynch mob to take into account.'

'Well, thanks very much, mister. Sure nice to know I can count on your support.'

'So what about it, Hastings?' asked Travis, gesturing back towards the cell, 'You choose.'

'I ain't got no choice,' said Hastings sulkily. 'You know that.'

'Great. And as you've co-operated with the law so freely I'm going to give you a reward.'

Hastings' eyes were bleak with renewed suspicion. 'Yeah?'

'How would you like to wear a gunbelt? Can't have you being shot at without some means of retaliation.'

'Mister, you sure got a winning way with words.' Hastings' voice was loaded with contempt, but the chance of sporting a gunbelt for the first time in his life was all but irresistible. He continued hastily, 'OK. It's a deal.'

A gunbelt, a six-shooter and a supply of ammunition were extracted from the sheriffs stock of confiscated hardware and arranged on Hastings' hips.

'You do know how to shoot?' asked Travis, almost as an afterthought, as he stepped back to admire the effect.

'Mister, I'm a farm . . . a rancher's son,' said Hastings, easing the Colt nervously in and out of its holster. 'You think I don't know how to shoot?'

'Just checking,' said Travis with a sideways glance at Truscott, He reached over to the hatstand, selected a stained felt hat which had been his own in poorer times when he had been unable to afford anything better, and placed it on Hastings' head.

'Not a bad fit – and enough to shadow your face as you walk through town.'

'Walk? But I thought . . .'

'A horse is no use if you're going to be on a train. It's only a ten-minute walk down to the tracks at the north end of town if you skirt round the back of Main Street. I'll show you the way. Just try to keep yourself out of sight.'

Suddenly Hastings seemed reluctant to move. 'But will you and . . .'

'Truscott and I will ride out ahead of the train. I've got the feeling that if something's going to happen it won't be too far from town.'

Hastings lifted the brim of his hat to peer at Truscott.

'You going along with all this?'

'Seems I don't have much choice, seeing as how Travis declines to make any arrests.'

Hastings was bundled out of the rear door and shown how to make his way round the back of town. Arming himself with the one and only rifle on the premises, Travis beckoned to Truscott.

'Let's make a move. We need to get you a horse.'

They were just leaving the office when Turner trotted up red-faced and sweating. 'Train's where she should be. Leaves in thirty minutes.'

'Fine,' said Travis. 'Mr Truscott will be leaving with it, He's completed his business here.'

Turner looked slightly surprised. 'Oh? And where's the kid?'

'Smuggled him up to my lodgings,' said Travis blandly. 'Safest place until sundown, I think.' He placed a firm hand in the centre of Truscott's back. 'Come on Truscott, no time to waste.' He led the way out. Truscott followed him, wondering why Travis had found it necessary to tell two lies to his own colleague.

Chapter Ten

It took Luke Hastings longer than anticipated to pick his way along the edge of town. This was largely because he felt obliged to stop at frequent intervals and look cautiously behind in search of the lynch mob that he was convinced must soon be hot on his heels armed with billy-clubs and pick-axe handles. In the event he encountered nobody and attracted no attention. At the northern end of town where the railroad actually crossed the trail that led back down to Drummond's Crossing he found the train halted by a large woodstack where logs of spruce and pine were arranged in ordered piles ready for use. The engine had been run around the train, with a single boxcar imme-diately behind the tender, while the passenger-car brought up the rear. There was no caboose. Up front the replen-ishment of the tender seemed nearly complete, and the engineer was exchanging banter with the fireman as the last logs were thrown into place.

Using a picket-fence that ran parallel with the track as a source of cover Hastings manoeuvred himself level with the boxcar. Some twenty yards of completely open space separated him from the train and there was no hope of reaching it unseen if anyone happened to be looking. At the moment the engineer and his assistant were occupied with preparing the train for departure, but there was no guarantee that one or other of them wouldn't look back and spot him. Hastings spent a couple of anxious minutes weighing the probabilities, and then decided that he was going to have to take a risk and damn the consequences.

With a final check that both men up ahead had their backs to him he vaulted over the fence and scuttled across the open ground into the space between the passenger-car and the boxcar. He flattened himself against the coupling waiting for the shouts that would reveal that he had been detected. But apart from the wheezing of the engine punctuated by occasional bursts of escaping steam there was nothing to be heard.

The woodstack was on the same side of the track as the fence he had just left, so there was no point in trying to enter the boxcar from that side – he would be sure to attract attention. Hastings contemplated the coupling that barred his way to the other side of the train, trying to decide whether it would be safer to go under or over. One thing was sure – if anyone came out on to the open vestibule of the passenge-car Hastings would be pinned there like a sitting rabbit. Without further thought he ducked down to scramble on hands and knees across the track. As he did so there was a rumble from the engine as the engineer tested the steam pressure, and the entire train seemed to shake itself, momentarily tightening the chains of the coupling inches above his head. For one awful moment Hastings thought that the train was going to move off while he was still sprawled across the rails, but the rolling-stock settled again – allowing him to complete his manoeuvre and emerge, still crouching, on the other side. He peered cautiously around in both directions but there was nobody to be seen. Here, the trees and undergrowth almost converged on the track, so he was completely screened from view.

With his back to the car Hastings edged himself along to the sliding doors. It would have been a help if the doors had been left open, but they were tightly shut. So now he had to use the iron handrail alongside to haul himself up so that he could get a toehold on the narrow sill that ran below the doors. Uttering a silent prayer that the train would not suddenly move off and dislodge him from his precarious position Hastings grabbed hold of one of the doorhandles and threw his weight backwards so as to draw the door open. As the door declined to budge Hastings was overcome by a wave of panic. It stood to reason that if the train was carrying a consignment of silver it would be an elementary precaution to lock the doors. Why hadn't they considered that possibility back in the sheriff's office? Maybe Travis wasn't as smart as he looked.

Cursing his gullibility at being talked into this vain enterprise Hastings launched a final despairing tug at the handle with his boot braced firmly against the sill – more to relieve his feelings than in the expectation that it would achieve anything positive. To his unutterable relief the door suddenly yielded to his pressure and a gap of a few inches suddenly appeared beside his hand. In the general silence the abrupt rumble as the door moved on its rusty bearings convinced Hastings that he must have been heard up front. If so, there was no point in being found spread-eagled against the side of the boxcar.

So it was all or nothing. He tugged again – and this time the door yielded the vital few additional inches which allowed him to slip inside. For a moment or two he crouched gasping on the floor, overcome with the excitement and physical effort. Then he stood up and approached the gap between the two doors through which he had just entered. He peered out cautiously, fully expecting someone to come along to investigate the noise. Then he clutched desperately at his head as if not believing what he was seeing. In the tussle to get inside, the hat which had been so kindly donated by Travis had become dislodged and was now lying crown up by the side of the track. If anyone should chance by, it would look distinctly odd. Hastings was just wondering whether it would be worth the risk and effort to climb down and retrieve it when there was an explosion of steam from the smoke-stack up front, a short burst of grinding as the locomotive wheels spun, and a jolt as the train began to move forward.

Leaving the door ajar so as to allow a little light to penetrate into the boxcar's gloomy interior Hastings sat down with his back against one of the wooden walls to compose his thoughts and allow his eyes to adjust to the dimness. His surroundings seemed reassuringly familiar – almost as if the events of the last three hours had never happened, and he was back to where he had started: just a few crates with the CMC monogram stencilled on them, while below his feet the wheels clattered and groaned as the train began to gather momentum.

When he had fully recovered his wits Hastings began to think about making his own position more secure. If the train was going to be ambushed, a shooting-match was guaranteed. In that case he was going to need cover so it made no sense to be sitting right by the doors. The crates were the only source of cover, of course, but they had mostly been thrown into the centre of the car. Ideally it would be better if he could wedge himself in a corner with a couple of crates in front of him for protection. Surely you could rely on silver ingots stopping a bullet?

Hastings stood up and approached one of the crates to test its weight – doubting whether he would be able to shift it unaided if it was fully packed. He applied his hands to the nearest uppermost corners and leant forward. To his surprise, the crate, although clearly not empty, yielded quite easily to his pressure. As Hastings slid it without difficulty across the floor, a question-mark formed in his mind. When he had settled the crate in position he applied himself to a second – with the same result. 'Now what in tarnation. . . ? he muttered to himself.

Then he tested each of the remaining crates in turn. All of them seemed to be equally lightly loaded. Overwhelmed by curiosity Hastings determined to take a peek inside. He fumbled in his belt for the knife which had proved so effective earlier in the morning and then cursed as he remembered that of course it had been taken from him back in the depot. He was standing there with an expression of total frustration on his face when he recollected that he was present in the boxcar as an agent of both CMC and the deputy sheriff of Virginia Springs. What the hell – he had status! There was no need to worry about not appearing to damage other people's property: a job had to be done, and he had been put there to do it.

He gathered himself and launched a hefty kick at the side of the nearest crate in an attempt to stove the plywood side in. The timber splintered where the toe of his boot had made contact. Disregarding the temporary pain in his foot Hastings rammed another thrust home and was relieved to hear the plywood shatter and crack. Now he was able to kneel down and insert the barrel of one of his six-shooters as a lever to split the side of the crate wide open. When he had removed most of the plywood, he shifted the crate around so that the shaft of light from the doorway penetrated to the interior.

As he had suspected, there was no bullion inside. Instead his hand encountered nothing but a couple of sandbags stashed so as to give the crate ballast. Hastings sat back on his heels and addressed himself with a self-congratulatory comment.

'No wonder they never bothered to lock the doors.'

He scratched his head in puzzlement. There was no

immediate explanation for what he had just seen, but one thing seemed clear: his own particular mission had been fulfilled, just as it had been this morning. Twice he had been posted to gather information and twice he had succeeded. And twice was quite enough, he concluded, after pondering his situation. The question of actually protecting the cargo no longer arose since there was no silver on board; and he was damned if he was going to risk himself for the sake of a few sandbags. Travis and Truscott were being paid for what they were doing whereas he wasn't. The temptation to call quits and extricate himself without further ado was suddenly very strong. Except, he realized with a pang, that his mission wasn't quite fulfilled. True he had acquired some valuable information, but it was useless unless it was actually conveyed to somebody. Travis or Truscott might make something of it, even though Hastings himself was baffled. But where were they – in front or behind?

His speculations were rudely interrupted by a piercing series of shrieks from the engine's whistle followed by the squealing of metal on metal as the brakes were applied. The train slowed abruptly, sending Hastings sprawling against one of the boxcar walls. As he attempted to right himself the train seemed almost to slide along the rails. Then from up front he heard muffled shouts followed by a crumpling sound. The train now came to a complete shuddering stop. Hastings ran to the doorway and peered out. The engineer had climbed down and was standing at the front of the train beside the cowcatcher. He scratched his head and then yelled up to his companion.

'Hey, Sam, come and look at this will ya?'

The other man joined the engineer at the front of the engine. Both men were pointing at something on the track, but from his restricted viewpoint Hastings could make out nothing. He was just wondering whether to

reveal himself and offer a hand when he became aware
that two men with bandannas pulled over the lower half of
their faces had ridden out from the trees beside the track-
side and were bearing down on the two railmen.

Hastings' first instinct was to shout a warning because
the engineer and fireman were too engrossed in their
inspection to notice what was happening behind them,
while the continuing hiss of escaping steam from the locomotive boiler was effectively masking the sound of
approaching hoofs. However, even as he opened his
mouth Hastings saw that both horsemen had drawn guns
which were levelled at the railmen at almost point-blank
range. As if to make it clear that they were intent on serious business one of the riders fired a shot over the engine.
The engineer turned to face them. Both he and his
companion raised their hands without any command
having been issued.

'What is it, mister?' shouted the engineer in aggrieved
tones. 'You the varmint who piled these stones on the
rails? Dang nearly wrecked my train.'

The riders had now come alongside the engine.
Hastings surmised that they must have issued instructions
to the railmen because the latter now lined themselves up
against the locomotive, hands in the air. But because of
the escaping steam and the masks concealing the riders'
mouths Hastings could make out nothing of what had
been said. Then one of the riders produced some rawhide
thongs from his saddle-bag, dismounted, tied up the two
captive's wrists and then bundled them at gunpoint back
into the cab of the locomotive.

Meanwhile the other rider trotted his horse along the
train. Hastings ducked back inside the boxcar fearful that
he was about to be detected, but the rider trotted past to
the passenger-car. Not daring to poke his head outside
again Hastings listened intently as the rider dismounted.

There was a clang as he flung back the gate to the open balcony, followed by another thud as he threw open the door to the saloon presumably to check for passengers. Then Hastings heard his boots on the track again.

'All clear here, Pete. Bring the buckboard up, will ya?'

The rider had now remounted and had positioned his horse almost level with the boxcar doors. Hastings stared frantically around with rising panic as the boxcar assumed all the qualities of a lethal trap, There was no point in hurling himself through the narrow aperture at the doorway, because he would be gunned down before he even hit the ground. True, he had prepared a defensive position behind the crates in one corner, but against two armed men his chances of survival couldn't be reckoned high. The best chance would be to try to slip out of the doors on the other side of the car and he cursed himself for not having had the foresight to open them when he had had the chance to do so undetected. Now, of course, there was no way in which they could be opened without attracting the attention of the man who was directly outside.

Reluctant to retreat to his prepared corner immediately, and thus lose all contact with what was happening outside, Hastings remained in the centre of the car, concealed from the gunman's view by the gloom of the interior but just able, through the doorway, to maintain the man in his line of sight. Moistening his lips Hastings prepared himself for the action he knew he would shortly be forced to take. If Truscott and Travis failed to appear, he was going to have to shoot his way out.

With infinite caution he slid one of his pistols out of its holster. The weight of the six-shooter in his right hand strangely failed to provide him with any sense of reassurance. Rather, it reminded him that he was about to take decisive action which he might not survive. Beads of sweat caused by fear compounded by the stuffy heat as the afternoon sun beat relentlessly on the boxcar's wooden roof, dripped down his face. He tensed himself, waiting for the moment when the doors would be flung fully open to reveal him as a sitting target.

But then came a momentary distraction. From outside he heard the unmistakable rumbling of a buckboard being manoeuvred into place. He could just make out the mounted rider getting off his horse to assist with the alignment of the tailboard of the wagon with the doorway of the boxcar. With the muffled commands to the horses and the general commotion caused by the activity Hastings realized that he had been given a brief chance to extricate himself. He turned about and groped for the doors on the other side of the car. Forced to reholster his pistol, he spread himself against the doors, feeling desperately for the handles that would enable him to escape.

The dire thought that the doors might be locked crossed his mind and was immediately dismissed: it would have made no kind of sense for whoever loaded the car at Virginia Springs to lock one set of doors but not the other, would it? Who knew? But as his hands slid desperately over the roughened woodwork an even worse truth dawned. *There were no handles at all.* Even as he frantically felt for some sort of fingerhold that would enable him to prise the doors apart, he found his mind dwelling with approval on the logic that had caused handles to be placed on the outside of the doors only. These cars were not designed for passenger use, therefore why would you want to open them from the inside? But there was no time for further consideration of the finer points of rolling-stock construction, because now the buckboard was in place and two timber planks were being extracted to facilitate the unloading process. The men were now close enough for Hastings to hear what they were saying.

'OK, Jeff. Push them doors open.'

Hastings spun round and dived behind the crates just as the doors were rolled back and the gloomy interior of the boxcar was illuminated by bright sunlight. The planks were now placed against the sill, and the two men swung themselves up to survey the interior. With no further need to conceal their faces they pulled down their bandannas, but with the strong sunlight behind them Hastings could make out little of their features. One of them stepped forward to the nearest crate and prodded it with his boot.

'Hey, ya see this, Jeff? Someone's stove it in.'

'Yeah?'

The other man joined him, and both crouched down to examine the damaged box. The man called Jeff fumbled about inside it for a moment, and then they both stood up.

'Whaddya make of that?' said the man called Pete. 'Looks like some son of a bitch picked it over already.'

'Kind of strange,' mused Jeff, 'considering that there weren't anything in it worth stealing.'

He thrust the crate to one side and examined the next one.

'Looks like this one's been picked over, too.'

Jeff stared down at the crates scratching his head.

'Don't make sense. But we ain't here to speculate. The orders were clear enough. We take 'em and dump 'em. Let's get on with it.'

They started with the nearest crate, manhandling it to the doors and then sliding it down the planks into the wagon. The second was dispatched in the same way. Hastings tensed himself in his corner. Only one more crate remained in the centre of the car, after which they would be approaching his barricade. The two men shoved the crate to the doorway, and as they stooped to manoeuvre it on to the planks Hastings seized his moment. Their

backs were towards him and they had no chance to anticipate his move.

He vaulted out of his corner and hurled himself
desperately at their two backs. Taken by surprise and
caught off balance they both pitched forward with the
crate which now slid down into the wagon while the two
men slipped from either side of the planks to fall between
the wagon and the boxcar. Hastings had thought no
further ahead than his initial move, but as the men
tumbled into the dirt Hastings, attempting to launch
himself to the ground, tripped against the leading edge of
one of the planks and pitched headlong into the wagon
right behind the crate.

The two men were stumbling to their feet with
confused curses as Hastings rolled upright and swung
himself over the edge of the buckboard. His feet were
touching the ground as the man called Jeff straightened
and reached for his gun. But Hastings was a second ahead
of him, his pistol already unholstered for the second time
in five minutes. And this time it really was a matter of life
and death. Without even aiming, Hastings squeezed the
trigger and waited for the man to fall. For a moment there
was total silence, and then as Hastings' finger squeezed
again, convulsively, his target's lips opened in a mocking
sneer.

'You have to flip the safety catch on those things, youngster. Otherwise they don't go bang.'

As Hastings stared at him and then at his disabled
weapon, Jeff kicked the gun out of his hand and levelled
his own six-shooter at Hastings' head.

'Make no mistake, mister. This one's loaded and
primed. You make one move and I'll blow your brains
out.'

Hastings' face crimsoned in an access of fear and
humiliation. His assurance to Travis back in Virginia

Springs that he knew how to shoot had skimmed lightly over the truth. The only weapon at the Hastings farm was an ancient shotgun, used to bring down the occasional woodpigeon or jackrabbit. Beyond that, Hastings' personal knowledge of firearms effectively stopped. He knew all about them in principle, of course, but had never had the opportunity of reinforcing theory with practice. Now he had been exposed as a total greenhorn.

'Don't shoot, mister, please.'

The second man, who had now positioned himself by his partner, shook his head in a snarl of anger.

'Let him have it, Jeff. The little trail louse was all set to gun you down.'

'Sure I'm going to let him have it. . . .'

Hastings watched in horror as the man's finger tightened on the trigger.

'But first I think we need to extract a little information. One way or another.'

'Mister, please. You took me by surprise. I was only hitching a ride back down the line. I ain't got nothing to tell ya.'

'That so?' said Jet holstering his gun. He brought his gloved fist crashing against the side of Hastings' face. As Hastings reeled backwards against the side of the wagon Jeff grabbed him with both hands around the neck, forcing his head back and threatening to throttle him. 'So you wouldn't know anything about those crates being kicked in . . .'

'I . . . I . . . I didn't mean no harm,' spluttered Hastings, desperately searching for a form of words – any form of words – that would earn him a temporary respite. 'I ain't stolen anything, I promise. Anyway, weren't nothing in them.'

'Yeah,' said Jeff, releasing the pressure a little on Hastings' neck. 'That's the point. But you ain't supposed to know that.'

'Come on, Jeff,' urged his partner. 'Finish the kid off. We ain't got no time to waste.'

'Sure. But not here in front of the loco men. Murder isn't part of this particular picture at the moment, remember?'

'So what, then?'

'We take him with us and dispose of him later. Plenty of suitable spots further along.'

Ignoring Hastings' continued protests of innocence they bound his wrists and flung him in the wagon along with the remaining crates.

'Good looking kid, ain't he?' commented Jeff as Hastings sprawled across the boards. 'Pity he's going to end up with a cracked skull.'

Chapter Eleven

As Travis turned to stride away in the direction of the livery stable, Turner's voice rang out behind them in a peremptory command.

'Hold it right there, gentlemen.'

Both men turned round in surprise. The sheriff had pulled out his six-shooter and was now levelling it at Truscott's chest. Travis frowned.

'What is this, Jed? We got business in hand. This is no time to be fooling with guns.'

'I'm not fooling. And I'll decide the order of business.'

'But . . .' began Truscott. Turner cut him off with a threatening gesture of the pistol.

'But nothing, mister. You're under arrest.'

'What for?'

'Manslaughter should do for a start – seeing as how you just confessed to it.'

'Hey,' protested Travis. 'We sorted that out. He told us it was an accident.'

The sheriff's reply was gruff and unyielding.

'Only his word for that, at the moment. We got a homicide on our hands, Nick, and until it's been properly investigated Truscott doesn't leave town.'

'But . . . you can't . . . I need to . . .'

'What you need to do, mister, is calm down and stop

acting like you were the sheriff of Virginia Springs. I may be getting a bit long in the tooth, but I still give the orders around here. You were out of line when you insisted on letting the kid out, and I ain't going to let the damage go any further. Any more *buts* and I'll have that star off your shirt – company man or not.' Turner nodded his head in the direction of the office door. 'Now get back inside, both of you – it's kind of public out here.'

There was a moment's silence, punctuated only by the sheriff's heavy breathing, and then Travis led the way back inside. Turner kicked the door shut.

'OK, Nick. Lock him up.'

Travis made no immediate move to comply with Turner's instruction. His face, which had gone deathly pale, betrayed no emotion other than dogged resistance. Slowly he raised his right hand and unfastened the star pinned over his breast pocket. Then he flicked it contemptuously towards Turner's boots.

'There you are, Jed. I saved you the trouble of taking it off me. I resign.' Turner stared as the star rolled towards him.

'OK. But you're still under orders. I said lock him up.'

Travis flushed. 'Lock him up, yourself. You're the only law around here now. You haven't got any call on me.' As Travis's hand moved to his gunbelt Truscott hastily interposed himself between the two men, obstructing any possible line of fire.

'All right, all right. Before this gets out of hand let me oblige you, Sheriff.'

He raised his hand to discourage any precipitate action and then entered the cell which Hastings had recently vacated. Turner swung the door shut behind him and turned the key which was still in the lock. Pistol in hand, he faced Travis again.

'I'm giving you a choice, Travis. Pick up that star and resume your duties, or I'm going to disarm you. You know the town policy.' He shoved the star back across to Travis with the toe of his boot. 'Which is it to be?'

'You're obstructing company business, Jed. If you won't let me use my judgement there's no point in me trying to work with you. You ought to be able to trust me and I ought to be able to trust you. I never thought time would come when you'd pull a gun on me.'

'I didn't. I pulled it on Truscott because you were in danger of making a big mistake. Now, answer my question.'

Making no attempt to pick up the star Travis unbuckled his gunbelt, let it fall to the floor and kicked it towards the wall out of arm's reach.

'Seems to me,' said Turner, 'that my letting you loose on a long rein has turned your head a bit. Maybe you need a bit of time to cool off and think things over.' He motioned with his still-drawn pistol towards the cell.

'Why don't you join your friend Truscott? Two of you can discuss company business together.'

He bundled Travis into the cell and locked the door again, pocketing the key. As Travis joined him on the wooden bench Truscott spoke.

'Mr Travis had a point, you know, Sheriff. For all we know CMC's about to lose a consignment of silver. You aren't exactly moving things along by locking us both up.'

'Maybe, maybe not. But what I do know is that the company lost a guard this morning and you killed him. Seems to me that that's legitimate company business too.'

'But . . .'

'Save your breath, mister. You ain't going to argue me out of my duty.'

Turner holstered his gun and set his hat more firmly on his head.

'So where's your duty leading you next, Jed?' Travis's voice was surly.

'Down to the yard to take some depositions from the men who found McCabe. Just routine, Travis – but the sort of thing you ought to have been thinking of instead of rushing off on some sort of wild-goose chase with your company friend here.'

He turned on his heel and walked out of the office. As the door closed Travis sat back on the bench with a wry grimace.

'Well, I really handled that like a professional, didn't I?'

Truscott drummed his clenched fist on Travis's knee in a gesture of reassurance. 'Don't take it too hard. It's kind of difficult to argue with a drawn pistol.'

'Yeah, but I should have known him better. He doesn't like to feel he's being railroaded and he's always been kinda touchy about his authority. I pushed things too fast.'

'No use crying over spilt milk. We'll have to sweat it out here for a bit.'

Travis raised his eyebrows. 'You're pretty cool, mister – considering we just sent that kid out to stop a possible hold-up all by himself.'

Truscott clamped his hand to his head in irritation, the events of the last few minutes having driven all thoughts of Hastings from his mind.

'Jesus, I'd clean forgotten the kid.'

'Makes it kind of worse,' said Travis with a trace of bitterness in his voice. '*You're* locked up facing a possible manslaughter charge, *I'm* locked up without a job, and we're *both* responsible for sending a kid to get himself shot. Real good day's work, and there's nothing we can do about it.'

Truscott considered this bleak statement for a moment, 'I'm not sure if that's entirely true.'

'What? Oh, great . . . . you got a fairy godmother who's going to let us out of here.'

Truscott smiled. 'Have faith, Mr Ex-Deputy Sheriff.'

He reached inside his shirt, fumbled in his waistband and produced the pistol with which he had rendered Hastings unconscious that morning. Travis stared at the gun in disbelief.

'You deceitful son of a bitch. You should have declared that as soon as you got up here. You know we've got a rule. If I still had my star on, I'd run you in for an infraction of the law. . . .'

Truscott grinned. 'Let's say I only just remembered it.' He reversed the pistol and offered it butt first to Travis. 'I'm formally surrendering it, as long as you use it to get us out of here.' He nodded towards the cell door. 'Do you think you can shoot the lock off?'

Travis took the gun, checked the chamber for ammunition and then knelt down to examine the lock. He chewed his lip for a moment.

'This cage is real well made. No way a six-shooter bullet's going to make an impression on an iron bolt. Besides, there's a risk of a ricochet. In a small space like this, there's no way of knowing where the shot would end up.'

'So we're stuck here, then.'

Travis considered. 'Not necessarily. If I aim through the keyhole it may disarm the mechanism inside – provided the bullet doesn't glance off and hit one of us.' He turned to Truscott. 'You want to take the risk?'

'Sure. What have we got to lose. Fire away.'

'And alert half the town. Like you were told, we don't allow firearms here. Any shot's likely to bring the whole town running – not to mention my ex-boss.'

'So . . .'

'So take your shirt off.'

'My shirt. . . ?'

'Sure. We need a muffler, and I don't see why I should completely ruin my own. It's bloodstained already. You know how much I earn.'

Truscott stripped off his shirt and handed it over. Travis hefted the pistol carefully and wrapped the shirt as snugly as possible round the gun. He looked at Truscott.

'Make yourself scarce, mister. I'm going to count three.'

Truscott stared around the limited dimensions of the cell. There was no place to hide.

'Some kind of joke, huh?'

But Travis was aiming the pistol at the lock. As Truscott hastily turned his back there was a muffled report, a sharp clash of metal on metal followed by a pinging sound accompanied by a cascade of plaster on Truscott's bare shoulder. Truscott spun round to find himself choking on a cloud of acrid gunsmoke. Waving his hand to clear the smoke Travis examined the lock again. The bullet had dented the metal plate around the keyhole and ricocheted into the plaster of the wall beside Truscott's head. Travis vainly rattled the cell door, but it refused to budge.

'Shit. One more try,' said Travis laconically. This time the bullet discharged with a distinct crump that suggested that it had lodged in its target. When the smoke cleared they saw that the keyhole had been completely ripped apart. Travis thrust his hand through the bars and pushed the tongue of the lock backwards without difficulty. As the door swung open Travis made an exaggerated gesture of courtesy using Truscott's shirt in the manner of a bull-fighter executing a delicate pass with the veronica.

'After you, Mr Truscott.'

Truscott grabbed the shirt, which now reeked of cordite. He dressed himself hurriedly while Travis peered out of the window.

'Don't seem to have attracted any attention thanks to your shirt, Truscott. Must be real good quality wool.'

'Was real good quality,' corrected Truscott, eyeing the scorch-marks with disapproval. He tucked his pistol out of sight once again, and pointed to the gunbelt which was still lying on the floor where Travis had kicked it.

'Your boss was careless, leaving that around. Why, anyone might pick it up.'

'Yeah,' grinned Travis, making haste to rearm himself 'I told you he was over the hill. Coupla years ago he would-n't have been so inattentive to detail.'

'What about that?' Truscott gestured to the floor again, where the star had fallen after Travis resigned. Travis stud-ied it for a moment before bending to pick it up. He hesi-tated, as if trying to decide whether to pin it on again. Then he put it in his pocket.

'Let's go,' he said, offering no chance for Truscott to comment further. But Truscott hesitated.

'What on, for chrissake? You know I haven't got a horse.'

Travis stifled a curse. Blade was tethered outside, of course – but that would be no help to Truscott. He pondered the problem for a moment.

'Look. You go out the back same as Hastings. When you get to the north end of town you'll see Wilkins's Livery Stables. I'll ride ahead and have a horse waiting for you there ready saddled.'

Having pointed out the route round the back of town as he had for Hastings, Travis slipped quietly out of the front of the office, checked to make sure that Turner was nowhere in sight, unhitched Blade, and trotted off down the street as calmly as if he were engaged on his normal duties. Meanwhile Truscott, feeling slightly self-conscious in his ruined shirt, made his way along the route followed nearly an hour previously by Hastings. Truscott had less reason than Hastings for being worried that he might encounter anybody, since it was extremely unlikely that the sheriff would have had time to publicize the matter of his detention. In any case, as far as most of the local citi-zenry were concerned his was an unknown face.

Nevertheless he was relieved when eventually the fascia board of the livery stables hove into sight. Emerging from a dusty path between two sets of buildings, Truscott crossed the main street and made his way into the yard.

'Deputy sheriff here?' he enquired of one of the boys who was tinkering with the wheel of a buggy that had obviously been brought in for attention. The lad stared at him and then pointed dumbly to a narrow passageway leading to the rear of the premises behind two clapboard sheds. Travis was pacing up and down smoking a cheroot which he stubbed out as soon as Truscott appeared.

'At last. I was beginning to think Jed had caught up with you.'

'Takes longer than you seem to think, having to skirt round everything.'

But Travis wasn't listening. He was already leading the way to a rail where two horses, Blade and a pinto, were tethered.

'I got you a real pacer,' he said, indicating the pinto. 'Won't be no stopping him.'

Truscott looked sceptical. 'Yeah?'

Travis unhitched Blade and mounted. 'Well, come on then. We lost enough time already.'

His eyes narrowed as Truscott climbed untidily into the saddle and the pinto shifted its weight impatiently beneath him.

'I might have known it – an Easterner,' he remarked as Truscott grabbed at the pommel. 'You ever ridden before, mister?'

'Sure,' said Truscott, making some surreptitious adjustments to the length of the stirrup-leathers. 'Just ain't used to these Western saddles.'

Travis made no further comment, but led the way out and then set a sharp pace towards the railroad tracks, glancing back occasionally to ensure that the pinto was right behind and that Truscott was still on his back. As the tracks and the adjacent woodstack came into view he held up his hand and pulled Blade to a halt.

'Well, we missed our train,' he said, as Truscott came alongside. They shielded their eyes against the sun and gazed along the track in the direction of Drummond's Crossing, but there was no tell-tale sign of smoke that might have indicated that the train was only a short distance away down the line. Travis muttered a curse.

'Do we have any chance of catching them?' asked Truscott. 'I know that loco only crawls, but even so it's asking a lot of the horses.'

'Depends where they're going to hold it up,' said Travis. 'If it's only three or four miles – and I think it is – there's a possibility. At least we know Hastings is on board.' He gestured towards the stretch of track by the woodstack, where a familiar object was clearly visible. 'I'd know that hat anywhere. Real careless of the kid to drop it like that.'

'Unless he left it deliberate like – to let us know he got here.'

'Right,' said Travis. 'Clever kid after all. Come on.'

They set off at a smart canter – Travis refusing to gallop the horses from fear of overstretching them prematurely. Truscott had expected that they would simply follow either the trail or the railtracks, but Travis had other ideas. The Truckee & Golden State Railroad had been a cheapskate enterprise from its very beginnings and had been inexpensively engineered. It consequently tended to follow the contours of the rolling foothills that extended down in wavy fingers from the high sierra, rather than cutting expensively through them on bridges and through tunnels. Because its route was indirect, it left scope for a pair of local experts like Travis and Blade to cut across the terrain and shorten their own mileage. Periodically after a detour over some bluffs or along a ridge they would regain sight of the tracks, but the train itself remained elusive.

'It's no use,' puffed Truscott when they paused on a wooded crest after some twenty minutes of pretty uncomfortable riding. 'We aren't achieving anything. And if this ride isn't killing the horses, it's sure killing me.'

Travis set his jaw. 'I was sure they would have stopped it by now. Looks like I was wrong.'

He was about to suggest that they give it another five minutes when something, caught his attention.

'Did you hear that?'

'What?' Truscott stared at him in puzzlement. Then from a distance he heard what distinctly sounded like the whistle of a train.

'It's a train, right? Or do my ears deceive me?'

They strained their eyes into the distance where they could see the rails disappearing round the edge of a craggy outcrop of limestone some half-mile away. But there was no train to be seen.

With no further word Travis led the way down to the tracks which they then followed. As they picked their way along the ballast several more blasts from the train's whistle reached their ears – sounding ever more urgent as they got closer. They rounded the final curve and Travis slowed the pace, uncertain of what he was about to find. To his relief the train was stopped about a hundred yards in front of them. He held up his hand.

'Best take it real careful,' he remarked to Truscott. 'Seems kind of peaceful except for the hooting, but we don't know what's going on.'

Rather than approach the train directly from behind he led the way off the tracks through scrub, thorn and occasional rocky outcrops until they had worked their way parallel with the locomotive. There was no sign of activity, but as they got closer Travis was able to make out a solitary figure hunched on the footplate bobbing up and down in time to the blasts on the whistle.

'What in tarnation. . . ?'

He led the way out of the scrub thicket and brought Blade to a halt beside the locomotive. The hunched figure, who had been pulling on the whistle cord with his teeth, staggered back as he saw the two riders approach.

'Hey mister. Get me out of this will ya? They tied my hands real good.'

Travis and Truscott dismounted and set about freeing the two railmen.

'Real nice symphony you was playing on that whistle, old-timer,' smiled Truscott as the engineer sat rubbing some circulation back into his wrists.

'Yeah? Well I can tell you it weren't funny, mister. Never knew whether we had any chance of attracting any attention – it's kind of a lonely stretch of country out here.'

Travis conducted a brisk interrogation to find out what had happened.

'Did you see a young kid on the train?' he asked when the engineer had explained the details of the hold-up.

'Mister, we couldn't see anything. We were trussed up like turkeys face down in the cab. But there was definitely a third party here and we heard the commotion when they caught him.'

Travis and Truscott exchanged bleak glances at this unwelcome information. 'Yep,' continued the old man, 'they caught him for sure – and took him off. Wouldn't care much for his chances, though. Kind of easy to have an accident round here, isn't it?'

Chapter Twelve

The wagon had only been rattling along for what Luke Hastings judged to be around a quarter of an hour, but the discomfort made it seem an eternity. With his hands tied behind his back he was unable to brace himself against any solid surface, so with every jolt he was rolled to one side or another, constantly fetching up against the sharp corners of the crates with which he was sharing a very limited space. It was also apparent from the uneven motion of the vehicle that they were following no beaten trail, but pursuing an independent course across country. Despite his justified apprehension about what was due to happen to him when, and wherever, the journey ended, it was nevertheless a relief when he heard one of his captors say to the other, 'This should do.'

Hastings was flat on his back with nothing but a view of tall evergreens overhead, but as the wagon stopped, he managed to shift his position to prop himself against one of the sides to give himself a clearer picture of what was going on. The man called Pete was evidently driving the wagon, while Jeff had been riding behind, with Pete's horse roped behind his own. It was Jeff's voice which had given the order to stop. Now he dismounted, looked around as though checking the suitability of the terrain for whatever he had in mind, and then approached the wagon. He lowered the tailboard grabbed hold of Hastings' legs and dragged him unceremoniously to the ground. Chafed by the rough boards and partially winded by the drop from the wagon Hastings lay curled at the man's feet. Jeff's boot landed a vicious kick in his ribs.

'Get up, mister. We got a job for you.'

Hastings stumbled to his feet with difficulty, facing his captor. As he had surmised they had not been following a trail, but had been travelling across country. He was completely unfamiliar with this terrain but they appeared to be on a timbered slope where the ground underneath was a mixture of sand and gravel. The tall evergreens all around shaded much of the afternoon sunlight. The wagon-driver had climbed down to join his partner. They surveyed the dishevelled figure in front of them. As Jeff fumbled in his belt to produce a Bowie knife Hastings thought his last moment had come.

Previous talk had been of skull smashing, but maybe a knife in the ribs would be a quicker end.

'Didn't reckon on having extra labour available,' remarked Jeff, handing the knife to the other man. 'But I figure we might as well make use of him. Untie him, Pete.'

Pete stepped across and deftly severed the bonds that were holding Hastings' wrists. Jeff drew his pistol as Hastings stood dumbly trying to massage some circulation back into his hands.

'OK, mister. First job, get them boxes out of the wagon and be quick.'

The two men watched as Hastings climbed back in the wagon and shifted the crates one by one to the ground. Conscious of the pistol trained on him throughout this exercise Hastings nevertheless contrived to work as deliberately as the gunman's patience would allow, in order to give himself time to marshal his disordered thoughts.

His prospects seemed bleak. Travis's assurance of riding
ahead of the train had obviously been a false promise,
since no assistance had materialized when the train was
held up. The three of them were now quite alone, off the
track, in country of which he knew nothing. Furthermore
he was disarmed. If he ran, his expectation of life would be
no longer than the second it took one of the men to cock
the trigger on a six-shooter.

He had just completed this sombre calculation when
the last crate went tipping off the back of the wagon
revealing a spade which had previously lain there unnoticed on the boards. Hastings surveyed the stout wooden
handle with a shiver, wondering whether it might have any
intended role to play in what was to happen to him next.
As he was pondering, Jeff spoke again.

'Git down, mister. Now you got the sandbags to unload.'

With an air of bewilderment, but not daring to ask what
was going on, Hastings set about extracting the sandbags
from the crates. His work was partially started already
since he himself had kicked some of the plywood sides in.
Now he extracted the sandbags one by one and laid them
on the ground. As he did so Pete slit each bag with the
Bowie knife and scattered the contents to the earth. When
this operation was complete, Jeff walked over to the wagon
and hefted out the spade. As Hastings watched in trepida-
tion he cast around among the trees for a moment until
he found a suitable area where a patch of gravel was partly
overgrown with scrub. Clearing the vegetation back with
his boot he beckoned to Hastings.

'Bring them sandbags over here, kid. We want them
buried.'

Hastings gathered the discarded sandbags and walked
across.

'Just dig a hole a foot deep,' said Jeff, thrusting the
spade in his hand, 'and bury 'em real good.'

Hastings took the spade and began to dig a small hole. When the men judged it deep enough the sandbags were folded and placed inside, the earth was replaced and trampled flat, and the vegetation moved back to conceal the recent activity. When this had been accomplished to Jeff's satisfaction he relieved Hastings of the spade.

'What about the crates?' asked Pete.

'We leave them. They won't tell nobody nothing except that we took the contents out. It's only the sandbags that were a tell-tale.'

Jeff now turned his attention to Hastings.

'Well, youngster, seems like it's time to dispense with your services. You got anything to say before you have your . . . er . . . accident?'

Ignoring Pete's chuckle at his partner's wit Hastings stared defiantly at his tormentor, having decided that if he was going out, he would at least do so with his head held up.

'You ain't got no call to do this to me, mister.' His face flushed with anger, 'I just stowed away on a train like I told you. I wasn't messing with your business.'

'Maybe, maybe not. But we can't take a chance on you blabbing about what you seen.'

'Hey, Jeff,' interposed the other man, 'Why don't we get him to dig his own grave first? He did a real neat job with them sandbags.'

'Because he's supposed to have an accident, muttonhead. You ever heard of a self-burying corpse? There's some nice rocky bluffs up ahead where we can drop him off.'

'Oh.' Pete sounded crestfallen at the rejection of his plan for auto-interment, but then his voice brightened again. 'Can I do it, Jeff? Used to be real good with the sledgehammer in the pen, remember?'

'My pleasure,' smiled Jeff, handing him the spade. He

motioned to Hastings with his pistol. 'OK, kid, turn around.'

Breathing heavily and conscious of the hairs on the nape of his neck rising in terrified anticipation of what was coming next Hastings turned slowly round. The muzzle of the pistol jabbed sharply into the base of his skull.

'Fine.' Jeff s voice was almost level with his ear. 'Kneel down.'

With nothing left to lose, and subconsciously figuring that a bullet in the head would be better than the repeated application of a spade handle to his skull, Hastings risked one final act of rebellion.

'I ain't kneeling for anyone, mister. I'll take it standing up – if your little pal can reach.'

'Why, you sassy sonofabitch,' Jeff's voice rasped in his ear, 'we'll just see how you take it.'

Hastings froze in anticipation of a bullet, but instead he grunted with surprise as a kick from Jeff's boot in his posterior sent him stumbling forward to pitch face downwards in the sand.

'That's it, mister,' said Jeff, striding forward to plant a heavy foot in the small of Hastings' back, 'now eat dirt.' He turned to his crony. 'Get over here and finish him off, Pete.'

Hastings sprawled under the weight of his assailant's foot. Clawing vainly at the ground in an attempt to lever himself away, while Pete took up a stance alongside his head and raised the spade high above shoulder level ready to bring the iron blade crashing down on Hastings' skull.

'Just like the old days breaking rocks in the pen, ain't it?'

As Hastings closed his eyes in anticipation of the blow he heard a report accompanied almost simultaneously by a sharp metallic clang. Pete howled an oath, as the spade which he had been brandishing aloft was twisted from his hands by an unseen force and sent spinning downwards. As it landed harmlessly on Hastings' back, Jeff recoiled in surprise, momentarily losing his footing on his intended victim. Aware that some sort of deliverance was at hand, and feeling the relaxation of pressure on his spine, Hastings squirmed to one side just as a bullet from Jeff's pistol crumped into the earth where his head had been seconds earlier. He heard a third shot fired from a distance and this time Pete, who had been standing shocked and immobile at the sudden intervention from forces unknown, clutched, screaming, at his chest to fall writhing across Hastings' prostrate body. Hastings was winded and hampered by the fall of this unexpected weight, but at least Pete's body offered him temporary protection ftom another bullet. As he lay there he could feel the pounding of horses' hoofs making a rapid approach, and then a sharp voice, which he recognized to be that of Travis, rang out.

'Hold it, Booker. Drop your gun and put your hands up.'

'Like hell,' came a snarl from somewhere above Hastings' head. Then Booker dropped to the ground, grabbed Hastings' hair and raised his head, painfully, off the ground. Hastings could feel a pistol muzzle pressing against his temple.

'You stop where ya are, Mr Deputy, or the kid gets it.'

The discomfort of his position now offered Hastings one small advantage: with his head being forcibly raised off the ground he had forward vision. Not twenty yards off, framed in the shadows between two giant spruces, Travis was reining in his horse, a smoking pistol in his right hand.

'Let the boy go, Booker. Ain't no point in mixing robbery with murder.'

'Ain't no point in serving any more time in the pen,

mister. You jest get off your horse and throw your pistols over here nice and easy. Or I'll plug the kid and then plug you. I ain't got nothing to lose.'

Rendered breathless by the weight of the body on his back and the constriction of his windpipe as his head was forced backwards, Hastings could do nothing but gasp helplessly as he waited for Travis to make his next move. He himself knew that Booker would shoot him without compunction, but did Travis? After a few seconds while eternity flashed past his eyes, Hastings saw Travis slide down from his horse. He stood motionless facing Booker and then, keeping his right hand in the air, slowly unfastened his gunbelt with his left. As it became apparent that Travis was planning nothing adventurous Hastings breathed again.

'Kick them guns over here,' yelled Booker as the gunbelt hit the ground. Moving slowly and deliberately so as not to antagonize his opponent Travis drew back his foot and sent the belt slithering over to where it was almost within Booker's grasp. To get it, he needed to reach over Hastings' head. He released his grip on Hastings' hair, letting the boy's head fall to the ground. As Hastings' face hit the dirt once again he felt a second set of hoofs pulsing the ground somewhere behind him. Booker must have become aware of the approach of a second rider at almost the same time, because before he could lay his hand on the discarded gunbelt Hastings felt him swivel his position in an attempt to deal with a second opponent.

Taking advantage of the moment of imbalance as Booker changed his posture Hastings rammed his elbow into the arm that was still holding the pistol to his head and sent Booker rolling into the scrub. The pistol exploded harmlessly as Booker's finger tightened automatically on the trigger, but Hastings had crawled from under Pete's dead body, grabbed the spade and hurled it at Booker's shooting arm, dislodging the pistol and sending it skimming out of reach. As Booker scrambled to his feet and attempted to draw his other gun left-handed Hastings aimed a flying kick into his belly, dislodging the other gun from Booker's grasp as well.

'Even terms, now, mister,' Hastings yelled, charging forward with clenched fists as Booker prepared to defend himself with nothing but bare knuckles. Truscott, who had ridden up to join Travis, aimed his pistol to fire a warning shot over Booker's head, but Travis put a restraining hand on his arm.

'Leave this one, Truscott, I think Hastings needs to settle something for himself.'

Truscott frowned. Booker was both taller and heavier than Hastings, so it scarcely seemed an equal match. But it rapidly became apparent that Hastings required no assistance. Dodging and weaving round his lumbering opponent he landed punch after punch on Booker's hapless anatomy, scarcely taking a blow himself, until finally he managed to duck inside Booker's guard to plant an uppercut that knocked Booker's head backwards into a tree-trunk. As he slithered senseless to the ground Hastings stood over him panting and sobbing with the exertion and the pent-up accumulation of fear and anger. When he had recovered his composure he turned to Travis and Truscott who had watched his performance in total awed silence.

'You two sure took long enough to get here.'

'We were unexpectedly detained,' said Truscott. 'Congratulations on your performance.' He pointed to the unconscious figure of Booker slumped against the tree.

'Told you I enjoyed a good scrap.'

Travis knelt beside Booker to examine him more closely. He tried shaking him by the shoulders, but there was no response.

'Looks like he's concussed,' he said, addressing the other two over his shoulder. 'I hope you haven't seriously damaged our key witness, Hastings.'

'Jeez, did you see what those rattlesnakes were fixing to do to me?' protested Hastings. 'And you're worried I might have tapped him too hard. You got some nerve, Travis.'

'Take it easy,' said Truscott. 'I think Travis intended a little humour.'

'Don't seem that funny to me,' said Hastings, massaging his sore fists. 'You two nearly got me killed. And for nothing. You know what? Them crates were empty. Some hold-up.'

'Empty?'

'Sure. Go over there and take a look. Weren't nothing in them but sandbags.'

He pointed through the trees to where the crates were lying scattered around the wagon. Travis stood up scratching his head.

'Seems that we need to take stock again, gentlemen. But let's deal with Booker first.'

They trussed him hand and foot with some cords procured from Blade's saddle-pouch and carried him over to the wagon. As they dumped him on the boards he started to moan incoherently.

'At least he's not dead,' remarked Travis. 'I'm sure he's got an interesting tale to tell. If not here, I'll get it out of him back at Virginia Springs.'

They examined the crates and then sat down to exchange information.

'Seems to me, Truscott,' said Hastings, 'that you've been barking up entirely the wrong tree. We come chasing after a pair of train-robbers and we find they ain't stolen nothing.'

Truscott shook his head. 'On the contrary, it's settled

everything.' Smiling at Hastings' puzzled frown, he continued, 'remember back in the sheriff's office we were debating whether we were looking at one plot or two?'

'Sure.'

'Well now we know. You just told us that Booker and Brodie never expected to find any silver in the consignment. So they weren't engaged on a separate enterprise. It has to be connected with what was going on at the depot.'

'Which explains,' interposed Travis, 'why they were paid up front. They never any expected any cut of the loot because they knew there was nothing to steal.'

Hastings scratched his head. 'Wait a minute, wait a minute. Now you're telling me that someone paid them to steal something that wasn't there. You sure you ain't concussed as well, mister?'

'He isn't concussed,' said Truscott. 'I'll need to check the paperwork, of course, but my hunch is that when I do I'll discover that the amount of silver allegedly in this consignment corresponds more or less exactly to the amount that's been filtered out over the past year or so.'

'Neat thinking,' said Travis. 'So it was simply a final operation to cover up fraud.'

'Exactly. Sooner or later they knew the books would be seen not to add up. So the accumulated loss would be accounted for by a robbery that never really took place. They were just unlucky that I turned up a day too early.'

Hastings sat back on his heels staring at Truscott in grudging admiration.

'Say, you really know how to put things together.'

'What I'm paid for,' said Truscott in gruff acknowledgement of the compliment.

'I'll quite enjoy discussing this in greater detail with the gentlemen responsible when we get back to town,' said Travis.

Truscott turned to him with a sceptical look on his face.

'Aren't you forgetting something?'

'What?'

'We're both wanted men. I killed McCabe and you damaged community property. I'm surprised the sheriff hasn't come after us with half the town at his heels baying for our blood.'

'He didn't need to,' said Travis with a trace of bitterness in his voice. 'He knows I'll come back without being chased. I've got nowhere else to go. Besides, our safety's guaranteed.'

'How do you mean?'

Travis pointed at Booker. 'He's our security. As long as we've got him we've got a hostage.' He glanced at the sun. 'Best be getting out of here. We need to find the road before nightfall.'

They deposited Brodie's corpse to join the still incoherent Booker in the back of the wagon, roped the two gunmen's horses behind, and set off to regain the trail back to Virginia Springs. Hastings drove the wagon, while Travis and Truscott rode in front picking out the wheel tracks that they had followed from the train. Within half an hour they had regained the rails where the hold-up had taken place. There was nothing to be seen other than the rocks which had been used to stop the train. These were now lying in piles by the side of the track where Travis and Truscott had helped to manoeuvre them so that the train could proceed. Half a mile beyond they hit the trail that led back to town. Travis reined in his horse, dismounted and waited for Hastings to draw the wagon level.

'Looks like the parting of the ways, youngster.' He pointed northwards. 'You can take one of the spare horses. Trail will take you back to Drummond's. Kind of a long ride, but you'll make it. I'll take over the wagon.'

Hastings stared in the direction that Travis was pointing to. Then he looked at his two companions with an expression of total disgust on his face.

'And miss all the fun in town. No thanks, mister. I'm coming with you.'

'Go home, Hastings,' said Travis sharply. 'You've done your bit. That's an order.'

Hastings raised his eyebrows. 'Yeah? Who from? You ain't got a star on your vest any more, remember?'

Travis clutched at the vacant spot on his chest where the star was normally pinned. A grin spread over his face. 'You're getting as smart as Truscott here. Must be infectious.'

'Sure. And anyway, I need a cold beer. Been promising myself one all day.'

Chapter Thirteen

The sun had set by the time the modest cavalcade reached Virginia Springs. Along Main Street occasional pools of light were cast through the windows of the few offices that were still open or through the half-doors of the saloons where the evening's business had yet to get into full swing. Travis directed Hastings to pull the wagon into the yard of Wilkins's Livery Stables, where one of the semi-resident urchins, alerted by the sudden commotion, came running out to investigate.

'Gee, Mr Travis,' he breathed, peering into the wagon under the uncertain light of the sole oil-lamp, 'looks like you been real busy.' He stared at the two bodies lying on the boards. 'Ain't seen anything like this since you busted the Connell brothers last year. You shot 'em both?'

'Half right,' said Travis. He fished in his pocket for a coin. 'Here. Take this and go find the undertaker. Give him my compliments and tell him I got a body here that needs attending to.'

The boy examined the coin, scarcely able to believe his eyes. 'A whole quarter?'

'Yeah. Told you earlier it was your lucky day. Now git.'

As the boy scuttled off they turned their attention to Booker. He was conscious now, but his incoherent mumblings had lapsed into baleful silence.

'End of the ride for you, Booker,' said Travis, untying his feet so that he could stand up. 'We're all anxious to hear what you've got to say.'

'That so?' Booker's lips parted in a sneer. 'You won't get anything out of me, Travis.'

'Oh, I think I might be able to change your mind about that. But there's no hurry. We know most of the story anyway.'

'Anything I got to say, I'll say to the sheriff.'

'Suit yourself.'

Truscott was beginning to show signs of impatience. 'Where we heading now? Your office?'

Travis shook his head. 'I think not. We have another priority, surely. Didn't Hastings say he wanted a beer?'

'Yes, but . . .'

Travis put his hand up to discourage any further protest. Leaving the horses they bundled Booker out of the wagon and hustled him along a side alley to the back door of the Silver Slipper. Travis opened the door and beckoned one of the kitchen staff.

'Get Ruby.'

A few moments later Ruby appeared and gazed curiously at Travis and his companions.

'Kind of unusual to come calling at the back door, ain't it? Why didn't you come in the front like everybody else?'

'Didn't want to attract any attention. My friend Mr Truscott here wants a room for the night. Can you oblige him?'

'Sure. But I still don't see the need for . . .'

'Do me a favour, Ruby. I'm tired – just give me the key will you?'

Shaking her head in bewilderment she disappeared to emerge a few moments later with a room key.

'Number four. You'll be using the back stairs, I take it.'

'Right,' grinned Travis. He nodded to the others and

they bundled Booker upstairs. Travis opened room four and lit the oil-lamp.

'Well, here you are gentlemen. You'll need somewhere to stay tonight. It's basic but clean. Mr Booker can vouch for that – he was here last night.'

Booker scowled. 'Hey how did you . . .'

'I make it my business to know everything,' smiled Travis. 'I even know what you had for breakfast and what you smoked afterwards.'

'Yeah? Well maybe we only had coffee and didn't smoke nothing. Are you saying you poked around here when we was downstairs?'

'Got it in one.' Travis turned to the others. 'Time for refreshments, I think. But not for Mr Booker as he's being so uncooperative. Let's give him a bit of peace and quiet to think things over.'

Booker's feet were trussed again, securing him to the iron bedstead so that he had no possibility of moving. Travis removed his neckerchief and bound it tightly round his mouth as a gag. With Booker immobilized, they went downstairs to the saloon and selected a table. Ruby came over.

'Everything all right, Mr Travis?'

'Sure.'

'What'll it be then?'

'Beers. And steaks.'

'Hey,' protested Hastings in tones of embarrassment. 'I ain't got no money to pay for all . . '

'Hush your mouth,' said Truscott. 'We're still on company business. It won't cost you.'

'Oh.' Hastings turned to Ruby. 'In that case make it two steaks for me. I missed lunch.'

As they waited for their orders to arrive Travis and Truscott ran over the events of the day trying to put everything in perspective.

'I still don't know,' said Truscott, 'why you haven't handed Booker over to the sheriff. Why not have done with it? We know how it all fits together.'

'All in good time,' said Truscott as the steaks arrived. 'Besides, why go hunting for Jed Turner when he's sure to come hunting for us. I used up enough energy today.'

'Always assuming he knows where to find us.'

Travis paused to down his beer in a few straight gulps. 'You don't know this town, mister. New travels real fast. I'd be willing to bet Jed knew where we were before we'd even sat down.'

Hastings was just polishing off his second steak when the swing doors of the saloon crashed open to reveal Jed Turner. He glanced around, saw where the three men were sitting, and strode over.

'Travis, you sonofabitch – you busted my jail. Now I'm going to bust you.'

Travis wiped his mouth with his napkin and leant back in his chair. 'All in good time Jed. Why don't you sit down. Have a beer on me.'

'The hell I will, mister. I warned you not to step over the line, Nick. What the hell makes you think I want to sit down at a table with you?'

'Because I've got a story to tell that might just interest you. And a guy called Booker who's also got a story to tell – once we've persuaded him to talk.'

'Booker?' Turner looked around the almost deserted saloon. 'I don't see . . . where is he then?'

'I'll explain in a moment.' Travis raised his hand to attract Ruby's attention. 'Beer for the sheriff, please.'

Turner, with a face that suggested he would prefer to be elsewhere, reluctantly pulled out a chair beside Hastings and sat down facing Travis.

'OK,' he said, as the beer arrived. 'You got five minutes, Travis ~ five minutes to convince me you ain't been trying to obstruct the law, otherwise I'm taking you and your cronies in.'

Travis leant forward and gave a concise account of what had happened at the train and afterwards. After he finished there was silence as Turner digested the implications of what he had said. Then he leant back in his chair, pulled out one of his favourite cigars from his vest pocket, lit up, and inhaled deeply.

'All right, so we got a real ingenious scheme to swindle Conglom. You want me to arrest Cormack.'

Travis nodded. 'Sure. Him and others to be named.'

'What's the charge and where's the proof. Don't seem to solve the little matter of Joel Bentham's murder, or do you want me to arrest Cormack for that as well?'

'Kind of unnecessary question, isn't it Jed?' Travis leant forward. '*When you know you killed him yourself.*'

Turner exhaled slowly. 'You got a real fertile imagination, Nick. Have you any proof for this latest flight of fantasy?'

When Travis spoke his voice had hardened, but he did not offer a direct reply to Turner's question.

'Time to call a halt to all this chicanery, Jed. There's been a missing link in all this, and you know what it is, and who it is. I'm looking at him right now. Bentham had only been dead for minutes when I walked into his office this morning, and Cormack couldn't have done it. I already know he was elsewhere. I guess poor Joel took the message that Truscott sent down the wire asking for all further silver consignments to be stopped – and he made the mistake of telling you. It would have wrecked the entire scheme if Booker and Brodie had had nothing to steal, so Joel had to be silenced – with his own paper-knife. Quick thinking, but kind of a ruthless way to treat a harmless old man, don't you think?'

Turner's expression was derisive. 'Pure speculation,

Travis. Pity you didn't spend the day doing some real detective work like I asked you.'

'Oh, but I did. Starting with this.'

Travis fumbled in his pocket and produced a folded scrap of paper. 'Know what this is?'

When Turner failed to reply, Travis answered his own question. 'It fell out of Jim Purvis's pocket in the cell this morning. Makes real interesting reading.' He turned and showed it Truscott who was craning across to see what was written. 'It's a bill of sale for a buckboard and horse from Purvis's farm.'

'So?' snorted Turner. 'He sold a horse and cart. So what?'

'For five hundred dollars? Seems kind of a high price for a horse and cart. But of course it included two other unspecified services – delivery to a spot where Brodie and Booker could pick it up near the railroad this afternoon, and, of course, Purvis's commission for keeping his mouth shut. It gave me the idea that, if anything happened to the train, it wouldn't be that far from Jim's farm.'

Turner smiled again, but there was less confidence in his voice as he replied:

'OK. So Purvis was involved. You still ain't connected me with any of all this.'

'Patience, Jed. I haven't finished. Flush with his money, Purvis was shooting his mouth off in here last night. That's why you took him in.'

'Hey, I . . .'

'I heard all about it from Ruby this morning in the course of the enquiries you were so anxious for me to make. I'm thorough, like you always told me to be.'

'Thorough, maybe,' snarled Turner, his face flushing crimson, 'but still a little too imaginative for your own good. There ain't nothing to connect me with Booker and Brodie, mister. It's all speculation.'

Travis shook his head. 'Sorry, Jed. I'm getting tired of this smokescreen. You cooked up a nice little scheme with Cormack to provide you with the nest-egg you need in lieu of the pension the township isn't going to pay you. That's all the motive you needed. And if you say you're not connected with Booker and Brodie, you're lying. It was you who set them up.'

'Will you shut up for chris'sake.' Turner by now was almost exploding with rage. 'I tell you . . .'

Travis raised his hand. 'You ain't telling me nothing. I'm telling you. I went up to their room this morning to have a look round. Know what I saw? Two of your cigar stubs in the spittoon. You were up there with them last night. Must have been a real meaty conversation if you had time to get through two half-coronas. Especially as Booker just told us the other two hadn't smoked.'

Turner staggered to his feet and drew his Colt.

'That's it Travis. I've heard as much from you as I'm willing to take. Stand up, mister, I'm taking you in. We'll settle this at the office.'

Travis remained motionless, his hands firmly on the table. 'I ain't going anywhere with you, Jed. Let's just say I'm afraid of meeting with an accident.'

'Then we'll settle it here, damn you. Stand up and draw.'

Travis shook his head. 'You're going to have to shoot me here in cold blood, Jed. I'm not moving.'

The sheriff's jaw jutted forward aggressively as he cocked back the hammer on the pistol.

'OK, so you're resisting arrest. You asked for it, Travis.'

As his finger tightened and Travis seemed set to receive a bullet in the face at point-blank range Hastings swivelled in his chair to launch the tip of his boot desperately at Turner's right hand. There was a deafening crack and an explosion of smoke as Turner loosed off the shot, but

Hastings' foot had just succeeded in deflecting Turner's aim. The bullet whanged into the panelling between the heads of Travis and Truscott, sending slivers of timber in all directions. Before Turner could fire again Hastings had hurled himself forward. As both men fell flailing to the floorboards there was another muffled report, followed by a deep groan. Travis stumbled round the table to where the two bodies were sprawled out. Beneath them a trickle of blood was oozing into the sawdust. After a moment of total stunned silence, the slender figure of Luke Hastings wearily disentangled itself from the frozen tableau on the floor. He stood up, gazed down at the inert figure, and turned to Travis.

'I think your boss just shot himself.'

Bright rays of sunshine were streaming in through the open window of Travis's lodgings. The room itself was spare but immaculately tidy, containing simply a bed, a washstand, a wardrobe and a writing-desk on which books and papers were arranged in meticulous order. The furnishings were completed by a sofa stuffed with horse-hair, on which Travis's overnight guest was beginning to stir. Travis himself was at the washstand, stripped to the waist, shaving. In his mirror he saw Luke Hastings push back his blanket to stretch his arms luxuriously.

'Past eight. I thought you were going to sleep all day. How are you feeling?'

Hastings sat up and took a moment to assess his own physical state before replying.

'Well, considering I've got a split lip, sore wrists, a sore chest, a sore scalp, a sore butt and a beer hangover, I feel pretty good.'

Travis chuckled as he wiped the remains of the shaving soap off his face.

'Yeah, it was quite a day.'

And quite a night too, thought Hastings as he sifted through yesterday's events, putting them at last into full perspective. Travis's studied air of inactivity had ended abruptly with the moment when Turner fell bleeding to the floorboards of the Silver Slipper. Doc Maguire had been summoned, but there was nothing for him to do other than formally pronounce the sheriff dead. With Truscott and Hastings as back-up Travis had swiftly collared Cormack and two of his cronies from the depot; they were then lodged with Booker in the remaining intact cell at the sheriff's office. It had been past midnight before Hastings had accepted Travis's offer of hospitality and bedded down on the sofa, falling into an instant exhausted sleep.

Travis went to the wardrobe to select a clean shirt. When he had finished dressing himself he walked over to Hastings, drew him upright and positioned him so that the sunlight fell on his bare torso.

'I see what you mean about your chest,' he said, examining the blotches that were testimony to yesterday's episode in the refinery. 'And you refused to talk in spite of the risk of being branded. Impressive.'

Hastings gulped. 'Yeah, well, ranching kind of makes you tough – like law-work, I guess.'

'Quite,' said Travis, one eyebrow slightly arched. 'Anyway, look here, I didn't thank you properly last night for what you did. You saved my life, of course.'

'Nothing really.' Hastings shrugged. 'In any case you saved mine out there in the hills. So let's call it quits.'

'Not yet,' said Travis. Feeling in his vest pocket he produced the star which he had taken off the previous day and had not yet bothered to re-affix. He held it out to Hastings.

'Here, take this as a token of appreciation. Or as a souvenir, if you prefer.'

Hastings hesitated. 'I couldn't take that. It's real silver, isn't it?'

'Sure,' said Travis with a grin. 'But what's the problem? There's no shortage of silver around these parts, is there?'

Hastings shook his head.

'Then take it. And, by the way, I formally release you from custody. In all the confusion last night I forgot that particular formality.'

As Hastings accepted the star Travis added, 'What's your first name?'

'Luke.'

'You can call me Nick, if you like.' Travis extended his hand. 'Glad to have made your acquaintance, Luke.'

As they shook hands Travis said, 'You know, there's a job for you here if you care to take it. I'm going to need a reliable deputy.'

Hastings affected to consider this proposal seriously. His admiration for Travis's qualities of courage combined with cool logical thinking had progressed in leaps and bounds over the last twenty-four hours, but he already knew in his heart that his loyalties and obligations lay elsewhere.

'Thanks, Nick, but I got a ranch to run. And the offer applies in reverse. If you ever get tired of being shot at, come down to Drummond's and give me a hand. The work's boring, but generally safe.'

'Right,' smiled Travis. 'I'll bear it in mind.'

'All of which reminds me,' said Hastings, 'that I've still got one unfinished item of business.'

Travis frowned. 'Oh, yes – you told me. Well let's see about it.'

When Hastings had dressed they strolled out together and took a leisurely breakfast. Then they made their way over to the shed where Hastings had been unloaded with the other crates the previous morning. Truscott was there, evidently making an inventory of the entire depot. He acknowledged their arrival with a cheerful wave of his hand.

'Howdy, gentlemen. Thought you was never coming to work, Travis. Easy life for some.'

'Mister, I've got four men locked up and four corpses in the morgue. Enough paperwork to last a year.'

Truscott nodded in sympathy and then turned to Hastings. 'It's in the corner, I checked.'

Following the direction of Truscott's gaze Hastings walked over to a corner of the shed. There, unopened and undamaged, lay the box with the precious Singer which had been unloaded with the others from the boxcar. Hastings turned back to the others with a grin of satisfaction.

'That's it OK. What a relief.'

'Train will be up from the Meadows in an hour or so,' said Truscott. 'I'll have it loaded in the boxcar for you.'

Hastings shook his head. 'Like hell you will, mister. It's going with me in the passenger-car.'

'But it'll be quite . . .'

'Truscott, I'm not letting that box out of my sight. I'm a day late with the delivery already.'

'Well, that's not bad considering the distance it's travelled from out East.'

'You don't know my ma. I'll be lucky if she doesn't try to haul me off to the woodshed for being tardy.'

'Some fate, for a rancher,' chuckled Truscott. 'OK. The passenger-car it is.'

'You bet,' said Hastings. 'and the company can pay for my ticket.'

Chapter Fourteen

'Carrying the security aspect a bit far, aren't you?'

Travis rested his hand on a corner of the seat in the passenger-car where Hastings was stretched out. The precious box had been loaded according to Hastings' instructions and was now placed with his boots firmly planted on top of it.

'Like I told you, I don't intend no mistakes this time. You never know what surprises Truscott here might be planning.'

Truscott raised his hands in mock surrender. 'I'm innocent. Give my apologies to your mother and tell her I hope she enjoys many hours of peaceful sewing.'

'Sure – if she's minded to listen.'

'Well, you can sweeten your arrival by telling her you're in for a cut of the reward the company will be paying for your help in wrapping up this little local problem. Two hundred dollars should be fair compensation for the delay.'

Hastings sat up in astonishment. 'Two hundred? But mister . . .'

Truscott clicked his tongue in irritation. 'Godammit, you farmers . . . er, sorry, ranchers . . . always want to haggle for the best price. All right, three hundred – but that's my final offer. Yes, or no?'

Swallowing his words, Hastings held out his hand as visions of what $300 would purchase from the firearms page of the Sears catalogue swam before his eyes.

'Thanks. It's a deal.'

There was a piercing blast from the whistle. The three men shook hands. As Travis and Truscott made their way out of the car Hastings settled down to compose a suitably modified version of the events of the last twenty-four hours with which he could regale his mother once the dust had settled. The train moved off, and as it made its leisurely way down the line the scenery associated with yesterday's adventures drifted past the windows almost unseen and unnoticed. At Drummond's Crossing later that afternoon Hal Cummings, who had taken charge of Streak and the buckboard in Hastings' unexplained absence, helped him with the loading of his precious cargo.

'Never knew you had a talent for disappearing, Luke,' he commented, as they manhandled the case into the buckboard, 'It isn't like you to go joyriding.'

Hastings drew in his breath. '*Joyriding?* Listen, mister, I could . . .'

'. . . Reckon you missed the big party, though,' Cummings continued. 'Engineer came through on yesterday's train dang near quaking in his boots. Seems he'd been held up. And what's this about poor old Joel being murdered? I can't get no information down the wire, so it must be true.'

'Yes, it's true.'

'Bless my soul,' said Cummings, scratching his head. 'Never would have figured it. Did you see anything of what went on?'

It was clear from Cummings' face that he was eager for information, but somehow Hastings was too tired to oblige him. A full account could wait until later.

'A bit of it,' he replied, with what was for him commendable understatement. And with that, Cummings had to be satisfied. If he wanted a further instalment of news he could always go and talk to the engineer.

Streak took him home at his usual invariable pace. Just as he had on the outward journey, Hastings appreciated the opportunity to sit calmly and re-order his thoughts. The farm would continue to be a twenty-four-hour a day preoccupation, but although it meant home and security, he found himself wondering for the first time whether it would ever offer him contentment now that he had had a taste of living life at a completely different pace. At last Streak made his way into the familiar yard, and as Hastings set about unloading the wooden case, his mother came out on to the stoop to watch him silently, with arms folded.

'Kinda late, aren't you, son?' was her only comment as he struggled with the precious cargo.

'Yeah, well, you see, Ma . . .'

'Luke Hastings, if your pa was alive you know what he'd say about you spending a night in that there saloon down at Drummond's – and you know what he'd do about it, too.'

'Ma, I didn't spend the night at the saloon.'

Mrs Hastings gave him a searching stare, almost as if she had suddenly realized that the boy she had dismissed on a simple errand yesterday had somehow contrived to return as a man. Then she sniffed suspiciously. 'Sure smells like alcohol on your breath. You telling me you ain't been drinking beer?'

'Well, no, not exactly. . . .'

Hastings waited patiently while his mother had her say on the iniquities of liquor, but her words flowed past him unheeded. Beyond her, he was gazing out at the setting sun flooding the distant hills with shades of ochre and crimson. And as he fingered the silver star in his pocket his thoughts took wings over the boundless possibilities of the West.